I0598999

A Merry Miracle
IN ROMANCE

Christmas in Romance Book 2

Melanie D. Snitker

A Merry Miracle in Romance
Christmas in Romance Book 2
© 2018 Melanie D. Snitker

Published by
Dallionz Media, LLC
P.O. Box 643
Boerne, TX 78006

Cover Image: Jennifer Pitts Photography
Cover Design: Shanna Hatfield
Editor: Heather Hayden

All rights reserved. No part of this publication may be reproduced, distributed, or transmitted in any form or by any means, including photocopying, recording, or other electronic or mechanical methods, without the prior written permission of the author, except in the case of brief quotations embodied in critical reviews and certain other noncommercial uses permitted by copyright law. Please purchase only authorized editions.

For permission requests, please contact the author at the e-mail below or through her website.

Melanie D. Snitker
melanie@melaniedsnitker.com
www.melaniedsnitker.com

This is a work of fiction. Names, characters, businesses, places, events, and incidents either are the products of the author's imagination or used in a fictitious manner. Any resemblance to actual persons, living or dead, or actual events is purely coincidental.

MELANIE D. SNITKER

This is a work of fiction. Names, characters, businesses, places, events, and incidents either are the products of the author's imagination or used in a fictitious manner. Any resemblance to actual persons, living or dead, or actual events is purely coincidental.

Copyright © 2018 Melanie D. Snitker

All rights reserved.

ISBN-13: 978-1-7327432-7-4

There are miracles all around us
if we only take the time to look.

MELANIE D. SNITKER

Chapter One

Savannah Wilson heard the light knock against the front door just moments before the dogs started barking. Apparently they had the ability to see through the wooden door and verify that an ax murderer was standing outside. Savannah sighed and didn't even bother to tell the dogs to hush; it made no difference. Instead, she opened the door and allowed her mom, Veronica, to enter.

Mom somehow stepped around both dogs while carrying a steaming mug of tea in each hand without spilling a drop. Nellie, the Sheltie, and Nessie, the Spaniel mix, followed Mom into the living room, tails wagging.

Savannah closed the front door again. "Mom, you don't have to keep bringing me tea." When her parents had volunteered her to housesit for their next-door neighbors during the holidays, it hadn't exactly been Savannah's first choice. But the Potters had few other people to turn to. They needed someone to watch over the house and their dogs while they spent Christmas in Florida with their daughter and her large family. Savannah had moved into the house the day after Thanksgiving, and Mom brought tea over at least every other morning.

She accepted the mug and took a careful sip. "Thanks, Mom."

"You're welcome." Mom sat on the couch and reached down to pet Nellie. She looked around the living room. "It is too bad the Potters didn't decorate their house at least a little before they left. It'd be nice to see some Christmas cheer in here."

Savannah had to agree. The Potters were well known for decorating their home from top to bottom every Christmas. They'd planned to go to Florida in the spring, but once their granddaughter was born prematurely, Mrs. Potter knew they needed to help with the three older siblings. They planned to stay until after the new year. Meanwhile, they couldn't take their two beloved dogs.

Maybe Savannah wouldn't have volunteered for the job, but she didn't mind all that much. She had no pets of her own back at her apartment, so it wasn't that big of a deal. And the money they were paying her translated into unexpected Christmas cash.

"It seems weird to see it without all the lights." She took in the bare hearth and empty fireplace. She'd attended many neighborhood Christmas parties here growing up. The food and carols were fun, but eventually Savannah would run into Baxter, the Potters' grandson.

When they were kids, she referred to him as her arch nemesis. He'd done everything possible to annoy her, and she'd tried her best to dish it right back at him.

So even though the holiday cookies and festivities were fun, it never did quite make up for the aggravation of dealing with Baxter. She remembered the time he'd pushed her underneath hanging mistletoe right in front of their friends, and then she'd had to endure being kissed by one of the other neighborhood boys.

Yes, she missed the pretty decorations the Potters usually had hanging up, but she didn't miss having to deal with their grandson. He'd moved away some years back, which was just as well.

Mom took a sip of her tea and continued to pet Nellie with her foot. Both dogs had curled up on the floor near her. "Have you heard how the baby's doing?"

"Mrs. Potter called last night to check on the dogs. Apparently little Sarah is in the NICU and likely will be for at least a few weeks. Right now, they're just hoping and praying she might be home in time for Christmas." Savannah could only imagine how hard it would be to see your tiny baby hooked up to tubes and machines. "I'm glad the Potters could go help out."

"Me, too." Mom set her mug on the coffee table. "Are you going to the tree lighting ceremony tomorrow?"

The town of Romance, Oregon had one of the most beautiful tree lighting ceremonies around. Savannah hadn't missed one in years, and she didn't plan on starting now. "Of course. Actually, Sweet Hearts will have a booth there with cookies, doughnuts, and hot chocolate. I'll be manning it at least part of the time."

Working at Sweet Hearts Pastry and Treats may not be a fancy job, but Savannah enjoyed it. What could be wrong with making and selling goodies that people loved to eat? Not to mention all the fancy drinks that put the small business on the Romance map.

"Oh, good! Your dad and I will have to swing by for some hot chocolate. I think it's supposed to be chilly."

"As long as it doesn't rain."

Mom stood up and gathered both of the mugs. "I'd better get going."

Savannah followed suit. "Yeah, and I have work in about thirty minutes. I need to take these hairy mutts outside to do their thing before I go."

"Have a great day, honey." They hugged and Mom left, leaving two dogs staring at the closed door behind her.

Savannah shook her head. "You two are pathetic, you know that?" She couldn't help but feel sorry for them. They likely missed their owners like crazy. Savannah was pretty much at the house when she wasn't working, but she doubted she made a good substitute for the Potters. "Come on, you two, it's time to go outside."

She breathed in the crisp air as the dogs wandered about the backyard. Twice, she had to whistle and call Nessie away from one of the many broken boards in the fence to keep the dog from exploring further than she should. As soon as she moved away, Nellie was right there in her place.

This was why Savannah couldn't just let them outside on their own while she tended to something else. She had to watch their every move. The Potters would never forgive her if the dogs escaped, and she'd feel absolutely terrible.

A few minutes later, she snapped her fingers. "Let's go, you two. I need to get to work. Cookies don't bake themselves, you know."

❄ ❄ ❄

The moment Baxter Reid pushed the door open, the scent of cookies, cupcakes, and coffee hit him hard. He breathed in deep. Though he wasn't one who normally went for fancy coffee, someone told him they made an incredible peppermint hot chocolate here. Everyone had their weakness, and for Baxter, it was peppermint.

He got in line and took in the variety of cookies and pastries in the display cabinet as he slowly made his way closer to the counter. When there were only two people in line in front of him, the sound of a voice jerked his attention to the register. He'd know that voice anywhere.

Sure enough, there stood Savannah. He chuckled and shook his head at the irony. He'd teased the girl mercilessly growing up, and they'd had many an argument yelled over the common fence between his grandparents' house and hers. Truthfully, he'd missed their banters when his family moved to Salem and he no longer visited his grandparents regularly like he used to.

He'd just moved back to Romance. Partly because he missed the small-town atmosphere and partly because he missed his grandparents. A lot of it had to do with breaking a cycle of somehow dating all the wrong women. Okay, and maybe a little of it was because he was curious how the girl next door had turned out.

Savannah hadn't noticed him yet, giving Baxter a few minutes to watch. She still had the same gorgeous black hair and eyes like pools of dark chocolate. She'd never been a petite girl, but even then, her little girl figure had been replaced with womanly curves. Savannah smiled brightly at something her customer said. It was a smile he'd often wished he could elicit from her instead of the constant look of annoyance he normally received.

He thought about all the ways he would try to aggravate her and wished he could go back in time and slap himself. If he could give his younger self some advice, it'd be that the way to make the cute girl next door notice him wasn't to annoy her ruthlessly.

The woman in front of him stepped to the side, making way for Baxter to approach the counter.

"I'll be right with you." Savannah spoke over her shoulder as she slipped a muffin into a paper bag. As soon as she handed it to her customer, she turned back with a smile on her face. The moment she recognized him, her smile faltered. "Baxter."

Her disappointment shouldn't have bothered him as much as it did. "Hey, Savannah. I didn't realize you worked here."

"I have been for about five years now." She shrugged. "So what can I get for you?"

"Someone recommended the peppermint hot chocolate, so I thought I'd give it a try." When she didn't respond, he added, "Please."

"Sure." She quoted him a price. He paid with a five and then dropped the change into the jar on the counter.

Without another word, Savannah got started on the drink, and Baxter moved out of the way so the next customer could approach the counter.

She was methodical as she worked, as though she'd memorized every step and probably never deviated from the exact order of things. That sounded like Savannah.

How many times had he teased her about being the over-careful goodie-goodie when they were kids? All of that time goading her had been a lot of fun, but looking back, he realized he might have gone a little too far. Especially if the less-than-enthusiastic way in which she greeted him was any indication.

Baxter had a huge crush on her back in the day. He'd thought of her from time to time in the years he'd lived away from Romance. Had she thought of him at all?

"Here you go."

Baxter accepted the warm cup and took a tentative sip. The chocolate-to-mint ratio was perfect. "This is great. Thank you."

"You're welcome." She hesitated as though she might ask him something. She covered it by picking up a napkin and handing it to him. "Enjoy the drink and have a great day."

"Yeah. You, too." Baxter watched as she turned to help the next customer. Banking the many questions he had about what she'd been up to in the last eight years, he left the pastry shop and stepped onto the sidewalk.

The biting cold air hit him immediately, and he was glad to have the warm cup of liquid in his hands. The temperatures had hovered a few degrees above freezing for several days. Thankfully, it should warm up a little tomorrow. Baxter had never been a huge fan of winter weather, so the less snow and ice, the better.

Although he wasn't sure which was colder: The temperatures outside, or the shoulder Savannah had given him.

Ignoring the whole issue, he drove to the other side of the square where the Romance Credit Union was located. He'd just started working there as a financial advisor last week thanks to his cousin, Caleb, who was the bank manager. Not only did it seem like a great place to work, but knowing someone was a plus.

Baxter had just stepped inside when Caleb waved him over to his office. He shut the door behind them, nodded toward Baxter's hot chocolate cup, and grinned. "So, did you see her?"

"See who?" Baxter knew full well who he was talking about but would not make it easy on Caleb.

"Savannah. She works at Sweet Hearts. Wasn't she in today?" He frowned a little.

What difference did it make to Caleb? Baxter took a long drink of his mint hot chocolate. "Yes, she was there."

"And?"

"I'm pretty sure she would've been fine had it been another eight years before I stopped by."

"I doubt that." Caleb shuffled papers on his desk. "Emmy thinks we need to set you up on a date. Just giving you a heads up."

Baxter groaned. His cousin's wife was a wonderful person, but her obsession with relationships was a bit much. "Yeah, I don't think so." Although his own choice in women left a lot to be desired.

Maybe Baxter was old-fashioned, but he'd always hoped to eventually marry a woman he was head over heels in love with, settle down somewhere, and raise a family where his kids could grow up loved. But for whatever reason, every woman he'd gone out with in the past seemed to want the opposite. He thought his last girlfriend, Reece, might be the one until she announced that she wanted to tour the world and felt tying herself down to one place would be a mistake.

When she told him she'd be unhappy in Salem or anywhere else in Oregon, Baxter knew it wouldn't work between them.

All in all, he doubted Emmy would do any worse choosing a woman for him to go out with. Still, the last thing he wanted to do right now was go on a blind date. "I think I've got enough going on right now, Caleb. But I do appreciate you and Emmy welcoming me back to Romance the way you have."

"No problem." Caleb paused, a mischievous glint in his eyes. "How'd you like the coffee? You planning on going back for more?" It was clear he wasn't referring to the beverage at all.

"It's peppermint hot chocolate, and that is a distinct possibility."

Caleb roared with laughter as Baxter left the office and went to his own desk. He shook his head, a grin forcing its way out.

The hot chocolate was reason enough to return to the pastry shop, but he probably would go back again even if he hated it.

Chapter Two

There were a lot of things Savannah loved about her hometown of Romance, but the way residents approached every holiday with gusto was right at the top. Every lamppost and store front on the square was decorated with white lights, gorgeous greenery, and red ribbons and bows. It was like something right out of a fairy tale, and Savannah was sure she could easily spend all day admiring the festive decorations.

She'd volunteered to take the first shift selling hot chocolate, cider, doughnuts, and cookies to customers at the tree lighting ceremony. Her boss, Jay Landon, was back at Sweet Hearts preparing more to bring in later. If past years were any indication, what Savannah had here would sell out quickly. Another plus to working the first shift meant she'd be free to watch the tree lighting without having to worry about customers.

Just thinking about kicking off the holiday season with the lighting of the huge Noble Fir in the center of the town square made her feel giddy.

Several times, Savannah caught herself scanning the crowd for Baxter. Surely he was just passing through town. She'd prefer that to worrying about running into him all the time. He'd probably make fun of her right now if he knew she was watching for him.

She'd just handed over two small cups of hot chocolate when Nicole Todd approached with her thirteen-year-old son, Tony. "Hey, guys! How are you doing?"

"We're great," Nicole replied with a smile. "We've been looking forward to this all week."

Tony nodded. He met Savannah's eyes and grinned before his attention zeroed in on the frosted cinnamon cookies.

Nicole handed over some money and said, "We'll take two of the cinnamon cookies, please."

Tony grinned as he accepted the treats. "Thanks! Hey, have you seen Kyle? I thought he'd be here by now."

Savannah glanced around at the crowd. Her nephew planned to attend along with his family, but who knew where they were. She figured she'd run into them later. "I'm sure he's around here somewhere." She got another cookie and handed it to Tony. "Give this to him when you find each other."

"Awesome!" Tony turned to his mom. "Can I go look for him?"

"Of course. Just meet us at the gazebo in an hour."

Tony glanced at his watch. "You got it. Thanks, Mom. Thanks, Miss Miller."

Savannah waved at him and smiled. She'd been taking Kyle to hockey practice for the last two years. Kyle and Tony had become best friends, and it was always nice to see them getting along so well.

"So where's Brent?"

Nicole smiled at the mention of her husband. They married in March and were as happy as any couple Savannah had seen. "He went to talk to Sam at the hardware store about an order while I get him something to drink."

"Awesome. Two cups of hot chocolate?"

Nicole shook her head. "Just one for Brent."

Savannah paused and gave her a funny look. "I've never heard you turn down chocolate before."

Nicole's blue eyes sparkled as she put a hand over her middle. "We're expecting a baby next June. And for whatever reason, overly sweet foods nauseate me."

"Are you kidding? Congratulations!" Savannah skirted the table so she could hug her friend. "I'm so excited for you guys. Is Tony thrilled?"

"Yes, though I think he's still getting used to the idea. He's hoping for a baby brother so he can teach him how to play hockey. I told him a little sister would be just as excited to learn."

"That's wonderful. But seriously, the baby doesn't like sweets? Are you sure there's not an alien in there?"

That had Nicole laughing. She brushed some of her dark red hair out of her face. "Hopefully it's a short-lived problem." She accepted the cup of hot chocolate with a look that was a mixture of envy and disgust. "Speaking of pregnancy, have you heard how Katie's doing?"

Katie and her husband, Mike, were expecting their first baby this month. With a due date of Christmas Eve, everyone who knew the small family couldn't wait to see if the baby would be born before or after Christmas.

Savannah shook her head. "I haven't seen her lately, but I need to go by and say hello. Last I heard, all was going well."

"That's good." Nicole lifted the hot chocolate. "I'd better go find Brent. Thanks again, and maybe we'll run into you again later."

"Tell him 'hi' for me."

Nicole waved and disappeared into the crowd.

Savannah released a happy sigh. Yep, there was just something magical about this time of the year.

Jay sent another employee to restock the booth twice before Savannah's shift had ended and she was free to wander around the square. The first thing she did was buy a German sausage dog for dinner since her stomach had been growling for the last hour. She took a bite and nodded approvingly. Yep, it was worth the wait.

As she ate her dinner, she meandered her way around the square, visiting with people she knew, checking out all the booths, and enjoying the general ambiance.

Her gaze followed a line of excited children to Santa Claus sitting in a whitewashed rocking chair. Even with the Stetson on his head instead of a red cap, she didn't think she'd seen a more convincing Santa. She could barely hear his deep voice as he spoke to the child on his lap who looked up at him in wonder.

Once the daylight began to fade, she headed for the center of town where the thirty-foot tree stood towering above everything else. Gorgeous red ribbon wound its way around the tree and red bows punctuated each of the green boughs. Last year, the number of lights on the tree had been spectacular, and she'd heard there were even more this year.

She spotted Jess Milne then. The sweet man was in his seventies and had recently gone through a knee-replacement surgery. He was sitting on the seat of his walker. Savannah waved as she approached. "Hey, Mr. Milne. It's great to see you. How are you doing?"

Mr. Milne patted his leg. "Doing well. Coming along, though sometimes not as quickly as I'd like." He nodded toward the tree. "It sure is something this year, isn't it?"

"It sure is." She noticed that he looked past her and his gaze locked on someone. He smiled. Savannah turned to see Doris Grundy visiting with her grandson, Blayne. Savannah knew that Mr. Milne had been interested in Mrs. Grundy. Since they both lost their spouses some years ago, Savannah thought they might make a great couple. Assuming he'd quit annoying Mrs. Grundy, and she'd give him the time of day.

Savannah covered a grin with one hand. "Well, I hope you enjoy the tree lighting, Mr. Milne. And I'll be praying that your knee heals completely."

"Thank you, I appreciate that." He gave her a polite nod. "Stay warm, Savannah."

"Will do." Savannah waved goodbye and then hummed to the Christmas tunes Chase Lockhart was playing from the stage. She tugged her jacket closed in front to keep out the cold.

"Wow, someone outdid themselves with the tree this year."

The deep voice came from behind Savannah, but she knew immediately who it belonged to. Baxter. Summoning a look she hoped was neutral, she turned to face him.

He wore a brown fleece jacket with the hood down. The color brought out the brown flecks in his hazel eyes. He smiled at her and then nodded toward the tree. "I've missed this. Holidays are something Romance has always done right." His happiness about the season was almost boyish. It reminded her of young Baxter.

It'd driven her up the wall back then that all the girls in school would go crazy over the fact he was handsome and had one of those smiles that could make you weak in the knees. Not that she'd ever thought about it. It was too bad he'd been so full of himself and so intent on making Savannah miserable. She might have succumbed to his good looks otherwise.

"Did they not have tree lighting ceremonies where you lived?" Savannah was curious where he'd been the last eight years. She couldn't even remember the last time she'd seen him. If possible, the man standing in front of her was even more handsome than he was back in high school. That wasn't really fair, was it? Especially when she'd struggled with her weight over the years. The fact she'd never been petite as a child didn't help, and add in that she'd always felt self-conscious in front of guys—and Baxter specifically—made her suddenly shy.

"Not like this. Don't get me wrong, Salem looks pretty enough at Christmas, but there's a lot to be said for our small-town charm." He gave her a winning smile.

"So what brings you back?" It seemed like weird timing since his grandparents were gone.

"I guess I decided I'd seen enough of larger cities. I've worked as a financial advisor for years. My cousin manages Romance Credit Union and offered me a job there."

Savannah tried to disguise her surprise at the news. "So then you moved back permanently?" Did that mean she would have to worry about running into him around town? The thought didn't exactly thrill her.

He studied her face for a second or two longer than Savannah was comfortable with. He finally gave a single nod. "Yeah. I rented a small house on the other side of town for the time being." He paused. "How about you? Besides working for the bakery, how have you been?"

Savannah shrugged a little. "I'm good. I stay pretty busy. My sister's son is thirteen now, if you can believe that."

She remembered when she'd first found out she would be an aunt. She'd told Baxter at one point, and that was one of the few almost normal conversations they'd had back then. He'd asked Savannah what it was like to be an aunt at the ripe age of sixteen, and she said it was pretty neat. While Baxter was the oldest in his family, Savannah was six years younger than her only sibling.

"That is hard to believe. It seems like just yesterday you were so excited about your baby nephew."

A little smile coaxed the corners of her mouth upward. "It sure does. Time flies, huh?" She tucked her hands into the pockets of her jacket.

Baxter cleared his throat. "Are you married?"

Now that was a question she hadn't expected. It took her longer than it probably should have to respond. "No, I'm not." He didn't need to know she'd never even come close.

Savannah had done her fair share of dating, but anytime it looked as though things might get serious, she withdrew. Currently, she wasn't seeing anyone, though she rather wished she were if only to be able to tell Baxter. "How about you? No wife?"

"I guess I never could find a woman who could put up with me." He gave her a sideways look, his eyes glittering and a little smile tugging at the corners of his mouth.

Stupid heart. None of what he just said or did was reason enough for it to beat erratically in her chest. Her gaze dropped, and she fiddled with the buttons on her jacket.

❆ ❆ ❆

Baxter knew he spoke his mind way too often. He couldn't quite tell if Savannah was more annoyed or surprised by his flirtation. There were a lot of things he'd looked forward to when moving back: being near his grandparents again, the holiday celebrations. And seeing Savannah.

They may have fought as kids and teens, but she'd gotten under his skin in more than one way. Seeing her now brought all of those feelings right back to the surface again. The problem? She didn't seem at all happy to see him. "You don't like me, do you?"

"What makes you say that?" Her eyes were on the tree in front of them as Chase Lockhart finished one of his Christmas songs.

Baxter had to step into her field of view before she'd finally focus on his face. "Look, I know I could've been nicer to you when we were kids. But it's been years, Savannah. Is there any chance we can put it behind us?"

Savannah shrugged and shifted her weight uncomfortably.

"It was the cupcakes, wasn't it?" The way her eyes widened told him he'd hit at least one nail on the head. "I'm sorry about that. I didn't mean to make you feel bad, but my goodness, they were horrible." This wasn't helping. Her cheeks had turned red, and she was pressing her lips together. "Everything else you've ever made that I've sampled was amazing. And I've heard nothing but great things about the pastries at Sweet Hearts. You're obviously an accomplished baker."

She blinked at him as though she were seeing him for the first time. "I appreciate that." She still didn't look convinced.

"What else did I do? Seriously, I want to know." And he did. If he had to, he'd apologize for everything if it meant she might give him a second chance.

"I've never been skinny." She held her arms out to her sides. "Not even when I was a kid. It was harder back then, though. You called me Miss Piggy once." The hurt his words must have caused her reflected in her eyes. "One of the mean girls I went to school with heard you at that party, and she teased me for months."

Baxter wracked his brain, trying to figure out when he might have commented on her weight. As kids, he'd thought she was cute. That later morphed into an admiration of her natural beauty both inside and out. Never once did he think negatively about the way she looked. And then a memory worked its way to the surface. He chuckled, which only earned him a startled look of disbelief.

"Savannah, I was referring to your hair."

"What?" Disbelief morphed to confusion.

"You wore your hair in pigtails all the time back then. Do you remember? That's why I called you Miss Piggy. You know, Miss Pigtails. I never even thought it might be taken a different way." It bothered him to no end that she'd thought he'd been so unkind with his words. No wonder she'd disliked him so much. Wow, he'd been an idiot.

She stared at him. "Seriously? Didn't anyone tell you that comparing a woman to a pig is never a good idea?"

He placed his hands on her shoulders. "I'm sorry, Savannah. I had no idea I'd hurt you like that. It was never my intention. Is there any chance you can forgive me and give our friendship a second chance?"

Chase finished his song and made way for Mayor Walker who stepped onto the small stage in front of the tree. Baxter moved to stand by Savannah's side so they could both see the proceedings.

After a short speech, the mayor flipped the switch, and the tree was immediately flooded with twinkling white lights. Clapping and cheers accompanied the transformation. The residents of Romance officially welcomed in the Christmas season as they sang "We Wish You a Merry Christmas."

Baxter turned to find Savannah grinning, the lights reflecting in her eyes. That was the smile that had his heart stuttering when they were teens. Yep, it still had the same effect now. He pulled his attention away from her face and back to the festivities around them. Everyone continued to sing Christmas carols, and Savannah was no exception. Baxter finally took in a deep breath and joined the crowd.

After that song had ended, he leaned in close to her ear. "Is there any chance you can forgive me so we can be friends? What do you say?"

She turned her head just enough for him to see her face. "I suppose there's a small chance. After all, Christmas is the season of miracles."

Savannah began to sing the next carol, and Baxter joined her, unable to keep from smiling.

Chapter Three

Baxter parked his car in front of his grandparents' house. It'd been several years since he'd been back, and nothing portrayed the passage of time like the lean of the wooden fence or the faded white paint on the shutters. He'd seen his grandparents every so often at family functions elsewhere, but only now did he realize how much he missed the holiday parties here.

When he'd heard they'd flown to Florida to help his aunt and her family, Baxter thought it'd be the perfect time to orchestrate a surprise as his gift to them for Christmas. Making repairs to the house would be something they'd never expect to see when they returned after the new year.

He got out of the car and glanced next door where Savannah grew up. How many times had they spoken to each other over that wooden fence? Most of the time, she'd end up stomping away angry at him.

He'd taken some satisfaction in getting her to that point back then because she'd looked so cute when she was mad.

Now he wished he hadn't been so ruthless. For one thing, Savannah looked adorable all the time. Secondly, it didn't matter how much he liked her; his actions had spoken a lot louder. He'd been that guy who drove her crazy. In fact, she was probably glad when he'd moved away and hadn't missed him one iota the years he'd been gone.

That was a depressing thought. He was glad they'd spoken at the tree lighting ceremony and cleared the air a little. Hopefully things would be better from here on out.

He could spend way too long overanalyzing things with Savannah, so he chose to focus on his task at hand. Today, he'd inspect the things he'd planned to repair so he could purchase supplies this afternoon and be ready to start in his spare time this coming week.

He made his way to the gate that allowed him access to the backyard. The gate itself was hard to latch again once he'd entered. He mentally added that to the list.

The back deck was in good condition. If he had time, and the weather cooperated, he might treat and stain it. He bumped into one of the deck chairs, and immediately the sound of dogs barking started up inside the house.

Dogs? Why were they still here? Seconds later, the hanging blinds in front of the patio door parted and two furry little faces stared at him.

The barking only intensified then as the Shetland Sheepdog and the little Spaniel mix flung themselves at the glass.

Baxter retreated down the deck stairs to the brown grass below hoping the distance would calm the dogs. When he turned around again, he found someone standing at the sliding glass door. No, not just someone. It was Savannah. Her hair was messy, and she was wearing a pair of sweatpants and an oversized cotton shirt. She looked beautiful, even with that scowl on her face.

When she reappeared a few moments later, she wore a sweatshirt instead. She slid the sliding glass door open while using her feet to keep the dogs from getting past her and running outside. She didn't even try to get them to stop barking.

"What are you doing here?" She crossed her arms in front of her and blew a small section of hair out of her face. "It's early."

"I came to check up on my grandparents' house. And it's—" he looked at his watch, "after nine, so it's not that early."

Savannah covered a yawn. "It is when you work at a bakery, get up before five every morning, and

Sundays are your only guaranteed days to sleep in." She planted a palm against one hip. "Or they were."

He cringed. "Look, I'm sorry. I had no idea you were even here. I just figured that Grandpa and Grandma had boarded their dogs."

Her expression softened a little. "It's okay. You couldn't have known. Yeah, they asked me to housesit for them since a month is a long time to board these little boogers." She cast an annoyed glance at the dogs, who continued to bark. "I'm just going to let them out so they can see you and then do their business. That barking is driving me insane."

Baxter nodded his agreement. The dogs flew out of the house the moment she opened the sliding door. They took their time smelling his shoes and the cuffs of his pants before getting pats on the head and turning to the more important task of finding the perfect spot in the backyard.

Savannah moved to sit on the edge of the deck, and Baxter joined her. She turned her head to study him. "It was nice of you to check on the place."

"I was hoping to surprise them with some repairs for a Christmas present. The fence needs attention, and I'd like to repaint the shutters and maybe stain the deck if we have good weather. Then I'd planned to go inside and see if there's anything I can help with there, too." He shrugged. "That was before I realized someone was staying here."

One of the dogs made her way to a hole in the fence and stuck her head through it. Savannah had to snap her fingers several times to get the dog's attention and call her back before she pushed her way through to the other side.

Yes, repairs to the fence would be a top priority. Not only did he not want Savannah or his grandparents worrying about the dogs escaping, the holes meant it was way too easy for something else to enter as well.

"I'm really sorry my stopping by alerted the security team and woke you up."

She offered him a small smile, which did more to the speed of his heart rate than it should have. "It's okay. Truthfully, I usually wake up about now, anyway. Sleeping in is good, but I don't like to sleep my free days away, either. I go to bed early to make up for normally getting up at the crack of dawn."

"Well, do me a favor and don't mention any of this to my grandparents. I plan to go tell your parents the same thing, and also Granny Mary."

She nodded. "Good idea. I'm not sure any of them are talking to your grandparents directly, but they might say something to someone else who would."

"Exactly."

"I think it's a nice thing to do. I'm sure they'll be surprised and pleased when they get home again."

Baxter liked getting her approval. However, finding time during the day to make the repairs would be tricky. He'd intended to come by in the evenings after he got off work and handle the repairs then. If Savannah went to bed early, that would cut his time by a good deal. "When do you get home from work?"

"Between two and three in the afternoon. I'm usually in bed around nine."

Baxter worked until five, but he would have to swing by the house and change out of his work clothes before he could get here. That meant he'd have maybe three hours each evening to work and about four weeks to do it in. Plus maybe most of the day on Saturdays. He could get it done assuming he had at least decent weather part of the time. "Any objections to my coming by in the evenings from about five-thirty to eight? Then I may try to work on Saturdays, too. I know it's not overly convenient..."

Savannah shook her head. "Don't worry about it. I'm sure it'll be fine."

He couldn't tell whether she was being honest, or if she was just being polite. He'd do his best to finish up by seven instead to give her a little peace. "Do you work on Saturdays?"

"I usually go in first thing, but I only work a few hours at most."

Maybe he could do most of the work in the house on a Saturday when she was at the bakery. He wouldn't mind the extra time spent with her, but he wasn't sure she welcomed that idea. "I'll try my best to stay out of your hair as much as possible. I don't want to interfere with your schedule too much." He gave her a teasing smile. "I definitely don't want to be the one responsible for your lack of sleep resulting in questionable baked goods."

She tossed him a look of warning.

"Too soon?"

A ghost of a smile appeared on her face. "Maybe just a little." She had to holler at one dog again and got to her feet before looking at him again. "If you'll give me ten minutes to change and put the dogs in the bedroom, you can come check out the inside."

With that, she disappeared and left Baxter sitting on the deck, smiling in her wake.

❊   ❊   ❊

Savannah closed the door behind her and listened to the sound of the hanging blinds clacking against each other. It really was too early to mention the stupid cupcakes. She'd baked and taken them to one of the Christmas parties at the Potters' house when she was ten. She'd only had enough batter to make a dozen and wanted to save every last cupcake for the party. That meant she hadn't had a chance to taste them ahead of time.

Baxter made a big show of being the first to eat one of her cupcakes. He'd also been the first one to spit it back out again.

Savannah had been sure he was just teasing her as always until she took a nibble herself. She could still feel the humiliation when she'd realized he was right. Somehow, she'd managed to confuse salt for sugar, and now all the neighbors knew her lack of baking ability. Something she'd spent a great deal of time and effort to rectify ever since.

The sound of Baxter spitting his cupcake out and then laughing at her was one that stuck with her for years. The shame of it all still warmed her cheeks every time she thought about it.

He was present and accounted for when it came to most of the humiliating memories she had from childhood. It'd been nice not worrying about it while he was gone. Now he'd returned, and she'd have to wrap her mind about the possibility of running into him around town again. Normally, just thinking about that would've made her feel tired.

But Baxter had apologized, and this time, remembering the whole cupcake incident didn't sting nearly as much as it usually did. She thought about that a moment and realized maybe they were making a little progress.

Knowing the ten minutes she'd asked him for would go by way too fast, she hurried to dress, run a brush through her hair, and put the dogs in the Potters' bedroom. Once ready, she opened the hanging blinds so Baxter knew it was clear to come inside. She then busied herself cleaning up the kitchen and adding to her grocery list until she heard the sliding door open and shut again.

The sound of his footsteps echoed off the hardwood floor in the living room. She could just see him go through the dining room before he disappeared from view again. Savannah focused on the dishes in the sink.

It was because of the faucet running that she didn't realize he'd come into the kitchen until he cleared his throat right behind her.

Savannah jumped, flinging bubbles from the dishwater into the air only to watch them land right in the middle of Baxter's shirt. She groaned. "I'm sorry." After snatching a towel off the counter, she pressed it into his hands. And she was sorry. Mostly. Although it would've been funny if the bubbles had hit him in the face.

The thought had her coughing into her hand to cover the chuckle she barely kept at bay. She turned her back to him so she could rinse her hands and found another towel for herself.

"It's okay." There was humor in his voice. "But you could've just told me I needed to take a bath."

She allowed herself to chuckle a little as they dried off. "So what's the damage?" When he looked confused, she elaborated. "To the house. What kinds of repairs do you think you're going to focus on?" Hopefully he'd stick to tasks outside the house. It'd be easier to avoid him that way.

"I need to repair the fence, but after that, I think both the front and back porches could use some work. A few of those steps are iffy." He looked thoughtful. "I was worried the inside might look as bad as the outside, but thankfully that isn't the case."

Oh, good. Savannah almost felt bad she was so relieved he wouldn't need to work inside the house. "Now hopefully the weather will hold out enough for you to get everything done."

"Hopefully so." He set the wet towel on the counter and then tipped his head toward her parents' house. "How's your family doing?"

"They're well, thanks." Savannah shifted her weight from one foot to the other. "And yours?"

"They are good. Still living in Salem for the most part."

"How'd they feel about you moving back here?"

He smiled. "I think my parents were a little jealous. They mentioned everyone coming here for Christmas next year like we used to."

"I'm sure your grandparents would love that." Savannah glanced at the clock. She'd need to get ready for the late service at church before long. It also surprised her that Mom hadn't come over with a cup of tea by now.

Baxter must have noticed her checking the clock because he cleared his throat. "I'd better get out of your hair. I'm planning on coming by tomorrow or Tuesday evening to begin. Would that be all right?"

It wasn't like Savannah could tell him not to make repairs on his grandparents' house. As much as she hadn't cared for him, she respected his grandparents. Keeping these dogs in the backyard had been a challenge, and poor Mr. and Mrs. Potter had to deal with that every single day. It'd be nice if the fence were repaired so their lives would be a little easier. For their sakes, she'd try to get used to the idea of seeing him regularly. It'd just be for a few weeks anyway, right? "Sure, that'll be fine. Like I said, I go to bed early. So as long as I can do that, there shouldn't be a problem."

He flashed her a winning smile that had his eyes sparkling. "Great. Well, have a wonderful Sunday."

"Yep. You, too." She walked him out. He got into his vehicle, ran a hand through his close-cropped hair, and then waved at her before driving away.

Savannah shook her head and sighed. This whole truce thing was going to make things interesting.

Chapter Four

Savannah walked into the house as soon as Katrina opened the door. She was there to pick up Kyle for hockey practice, and it was one of the few days where the sisters got to visit for a few minutes.

Katrina motioned to the staircase. "Kyle is upstairs taking a shower before he changes into his uniform."

Savannah's brows rose, and she fought for a neutral expression. "He does know he's going to hockey practice where he'll get horribly sweaty and need another shower when he gets home, right?"

While Katrina was not a single mother, her husband, Don, traveled all week and was only home during the weekend. Savannah knew how hard that was on her older sister sometimes. Years ago, she'd volunteered to take Kyle to an activity once a week just to give Katrina a well-deserved break. Once he started roller hockey, that became Savannah's time with her nephew. Katrina always made it to his games, though.

"Yes, he's fully aware of that." Katrina led the way to the couch in the living room where they both sat. "It turns out a teammate has a younger sister who said she was coming to practice today."

"Oh, really?" Savannah chuckled and made a mental note to watch for the girl tonight. When had her little nephew gotten old enough to notice girls? "I'll be sure to report back if there's anything worth mentioning."

"Sounds good." Katrina shifted on the couch. "Speaking of reporting, I thought I saw Baxter at the Christmas tree lighting ceremony." She said it casually, but there was nothing casual about the way she watched Savannah and waited for more information.

"Yeah, he moved back to Romance again." Katrina was one of the few people that knew about the torturous interactions between her and Baxter.

"Ooh, you guys have been talking?" Her eyes glittered with interest.

Savannah flashed her a look of warning. "It's not like that. Trust me. He wants to make some repairs on the Potters' house to surprise them when they get back. He came by on Sunday and didn't realize I was housesitting."

"Wow. How do you feel about that?"

"I think it's nice of him to do that for his grandparents. Trust me, that backyard fence is in serious need of repairs. How their dogs haven't escaped before now is beyond me." Savannah kicked her shoes off and brought her feet up to sit cross-legged on the couch.

"That's not what I mean." Katrina chuckled.

"Yeah, I know." Savannah sighed. "I had every intention of ignoring him. Avoiding him."

Katrina looked even more interested. "I take it that's not going according to plan?"

"It's pretty hard to give someone the cold shoulder when he's apologized for everything. He's called a truce."

She glanced at Katrina and found her trying not to laugh.

"Seriously?" Savannah gave her a playful shove. "What's so funny?"

"You realize that you two are now officially frenemies." When Savannah rolled her eyes, she continued, "Baxter lacked a lot of tact, but I don't think he was ever as bad as he seemed. In fact, I think he might have liked you back then. It's nice that you two have a chance to start over."

Savannah shook her head. "There's no way he liked me. Hated is more like it." She knew boys could tease a girl they liked. But even considering the misunderstanding surrounding the Miss Piggy incident, they'd never had moments where they connected. It was always like going into battle with him. Frankly, the endless sparring got old.

She'd just focus on the truce and hopefully a peaceful coexistence when needed. Baxter would finish the repairs, Savannah would go back to her apartment, and their run-ins would be few and far between after that.

❄ ❄ ❄

Baxter held another picket and nailed it into place. Originally, he hadn't intended to construct a nearly new fence. But once he marked the rotten boards and those broken at the bottom, more were going to need to be replaced than not. He wasn't a perfectionist, but even he would've been annoyed by the strange combination of weathered gray pickets mixed in with the bright new ones.

He ended up having to order enough pickets to go all the way around the yard and have them delivered. Apparently December wasn't a popular time to build a wooden fence. Who knew? Baxter was finally starting on the work today. Thankfully, they had a nice break in the rain so he could focus on the fence without getting soaked.

So far, he'd yet to see Savannah. Granted, he hadn't spent as much time in the backyard as he thought he would. But still, the disappointment surprised him.

He was just about to give up on seeing her today, too, when the sliding glass door opened and she stepped onto the porch. "Nessie is whining at the door. Is it okay if I let them out?"

"Sure." He moved to position a couple of pickets in place so there was no exit for the dogs to escape.

She nodded once, disappeared for a moment, and then reappeared wearing a coat. Both dogs flew past her to race toward him. Several barks and tail wags later, they were off to sniff around the yard.

Savannah seemed to hesitate on the porch before slipping her hands into her coat pockets and walking down the stairs to the grass.

"Wow, the fence is going to look great." She motioned to the stacks of pickets. "I take it you decided to replace the whole thing?"

"I think it needs it. It'll look a lot nicer, don't you agree?"

"I do." She studied the pickets he was working on now. "Would it be easier to just remove a whole section of the fence first?"

"It would, but then you'd have to walk the dogs on a leash. This way, when I'm done, there won't be any gaps for them to escape through. Well, no new ones, anyway." He smiled at her.

She looked surprised. "I appreciate that. Your grandparents will be thrilled when they see this."

The pair of dogs explored the pile of wood with great interest. Nellie tried to climb it as though she were a goat. Baxter and Savannah laughed. Savannah took out her cell phone and snapped a picture.

"To show them after they get back," she explained. "Mrs. Potter will get a kick out of that."

"Grandma always has loved her dogs." Baxter couldn't remember a time when they didn't have at least one.

"Your grandfather loves them, too. He just likes to pretend otherwise."

Baxter laughed again. She was right. "Grandpa would complain about the dogs all the time, but then he was the one who slipped bits of food to them under the table. Or he would go to the pet store to buy a box of dog treats, put a bow on them, and place them under the tree. Anyone who knows him also knows just how soft-hearted he really is."

"Most definitely." Savannah smiled. "Your grandparents really are kind people."

"Yeah, they are." He nodded toward the fence. "That's why I want to do this for them. Goodness knows they put up with a lot from me growing up."

"Isn't that the truth." She shot him a teasing look, one he wasn't used to seeing. "I think it's a nice thought."

Just for a moment, Savannah's expression was open. Baxter wished he'd spoken to her and called a truce years ago, especially if it meant she looked at him this way more often. "Well, it was nice of you to house sit for them. I know they are much more at ease knowing the dogs are here at the home they are familiar with instead of sitting in a kennel for a month."

Savannah shrugged. "I don't mind. The house is nice and quiet, unlike my apartment. The neighbor above me works weird hours and isn't quiet about clomping across the floor when he gets home. Then the neighbor on one side likes to yell at her kids. A lot. Oh, and they yell back. So yeah, I've enjoyed the peace here." She hesitated. "The Potters are paying me to stay here, in case you thought I was just doing it out of the kindness of my heart."

She wasn't fooling anyone. Baxter didn't doubt she would've agreed even if they hadn't paid her. In fact, he knew it was Grandma who'd insisted on paying her no matter what. Besides, her apartment sounded terrible.

"I hate to hear where you're living is so annoying. Any plans on moving somewhere else?"

"It's just three blocks from Sweet Hearts, and the rent is pretty hard to beat."

Most likely because of the neighbors, but he said nothing. He was enjoying this easy conversation with her.

One dog stuck her head through a hole in a fence slat that he hadn't been able to repair yet. Savannah snapped her fingers to get the dog's attention before turning back to him. "Any idea how long it'll take to fix the entire fence? I imagine it'll take a lot more work than you'd originally planned on."

He couldn't tell whether she was asking out of curiosity, or disappointed that he might be coming by in the evenings more. He decided to go with the first. "I'm not sure. A lot of it will depend on the weather. If I can get some clear, rain-free days, it'll go faster."

She nodded. "I guess I should let you get back to it. It really does look nice." She offered him a small smile before calling the dogs to her and leading them back inside the house.

Baxter tried to focus on replacing the fence. It wasn't easy when his mind kept going back over one of the first normal conversations he'd had with Savannah in a long time. Hopefully the first of many.

Chapter Five

Poor Baxter. When Savannah got home from the bakery Tuesday evening, she found the guy outside working on the fence in the rain. Granted, it was more of a mist than anything. But still, it was a cold mist, and it couldn't be fun.

She changed into warm sweatpants and a baggy sweatshirt before letting the dogs outside to do their business. Baxter looked up from the picket he was nailing and gave her a friendly wave.

With the hood of his green rain jacket pulled up over his head, it was hard to see his face. Savannah imagined that grin of his and nearly smiled in return. She pushed the thought away. The dogs, who weren't too keen on staying out in the rain, ran past her and back inside the house, their wet paws slipping on the hardwood floor.

Savannah tried to watch one of her favorite TV shows for a while. When that didn't work, she got on her laptop to check her e-mail. The whole time, she kept thinking about poor Baxter out there in the rain.

"This is ridiculous." She rolled her eyes at herself. The last person she should feel sorry for was Baxter. Yet, every time she looked out the window and saw him working tirelessly, her heart squeezed a little.

It wasn't easy, but she had to admit that, as awful as he was to her growing up, he'd always been kind and thoughtful to his grandparents.

She finally groaned and dragged herself to the kitchen to make two mugs of hot chocolate. She would've added peppermint to them if she could've found some. Truthfully, the food choices were less than stellar. Savannah had bought little for herself, and it made sense that Mr. and Mrs. Potter wouldn't want food to go to waste during their month-long trip.

Savannah put her boots on, slipped through the sliding glass door without the dogs escaping, and closed it again behind her. "Hey, Baxter!"

The hammering stopped, and he turned to face her, looking surprised.

"You up for a hot chocolate break?"

His face broke into a grin. He set the hammer down and jogged across the backyard. "You are an angel."

He ditched his wet gloves as soon as he was under the protection of the covered porch. He reached for a mug, cupped it in his hands, and took a sip.

Savannah hid a smile with her own mug. "It's nothing like the cocoa you can get at Sweet Hearts, but packets were all I had on hand."

"Are you kidding?" He flexed one hand and then another. Both were red from the cold. "It tastes amazing to me."

She sank into one of the two chairs on the porch, and Baxter claimed the other one. They sat in silence as they sipped their hot chocolate.

He'd finished the whole back of the fence and most of one side. He only had the other side to go and then the sections next to the gates at the front. "Are you planning on replacing the gates? Or leaving them as they are?"

"You know, I've been wondering the same thing. But I think I may leave them. I'll ask Grandpa in January and see if he wants to get new ones. As long as the rest of the fence is replaced, I don't think the gates will look too bad. Do you?"

"I think it'll look great either way."

He seemed content with her answer. He finished his hot chocolate and set the empty mug on the wicker table between them. "I guess I should get back after it. Thanks for the much-needed break."

There was no missing the hesitancy in his voice. He stood, flipped his hood back over his head, put his gloves on, and clomped back out into the yard.

Savannah took their mugs inside. She thought about turning on a Christmas movie but didn't even get as far as the living room.

Just thinking about him out there working in the rain while she was warm and dry inside had her feeling guilty. The sooner he got done with the fence, the sooner he could work on the porch or something else that had more shelter. Oh, and the sooner he'd be on his way, too. Which, of course, was the sole reason why she donned her boots again and withdrew a rain jacket from the hall closet.

She made it most of the way across the yard before Baxter noticed her. His brows rose in surprise.

"Hey. What are you doing out here?" He glanced at the back door as though he half expected her to run inside again.

"You looked like you could use some help out here."

He blinked at her. "You're seriously offering to help me? In the rain."

Savannah released a deep sigh. "I figured it was practically inhumane to leave you out here by yourself. I can't even enjoy a good cup of tea or read a book without feeling guilty."

She could tell by his expression he wasn't sure whether to take her seriously. Only when she gave him a small smile did he grin in response. "If you insist."

"I do. Besides, the quicker we get all this done, the faster you'll be out of my hair."

"Right. Of course." He chuckled. "In that case, take these." He handed her a box of nails.

She hefted it in her hand. "That's it?"

"You can help me hold the planks in place, too."

"Oh, well, that's better."

❋   ❋   ❋

When Savannah first offered to help him, Baxter wasn't sure what her motivations were. She acted like she was joking about getting him out of her hair. He wasn't so sure that was true, though. Even still, they fell into an easy pattern as they removed the old fence planks and replaced them with new ones. While he did all the hammering, just having her there to hand him the nails and help hold the boards made all the difference.

It wasn't just having help, though. It was the company. The evenings he'd been working before now had been long ones with nothing but the sounds of hammering and his own humming or whistling to fill his ears.

Savannah's company made it all a whole lot better. They didn't talk a lot, and when they did, they stuck to mundane conversation. But her pretty voice, soft laughter, and the subtle scent of vanilla that sometimes wafted his way made the day more pleasant.

Besides, she looked super adorable in sweatpants, boots, and a rain jacket that was far too big for her. It must be Grandpa's. He wished he could sneak a photo of her with his phone, but she'd probably smack him with one of the fence planks.

They worked together until the sun had nearly disappeared and called it a day just before five.

"You know," he began as they put the tools away, "it is time for dinner. Any chance you might want to share said meal?"

He'd known the answer to that question the moment it left his lips. She shook her head.

"Come on. Not even if I'm buying?"

"I appreciate the offer, but no, thank you." There was a flash of pain on Savannah's face before she schooled her features. She motioned toward the house. "I have every intention of taking a hot shower to thaw out, nuking a Hot Pocket, and going to bed."

Baxter feigned astonishment. "You're seriously putting down my offer of food for a Hot Pocket? That barely qualifies."

"Goodness, yer making great progress on the fence." There was no missing the Scottish lilt of

Granny Mary next door. They couldn't see but snatches of her bright red umbrella through the slats in the fence. "Baxter, yer grandparents are gonna be so surprised."

He exchanged a smile with Savannah. "I sure hope so, Granny Mary. Thanks again for promising to not say a thing to them."

"Yer secret's safe with me. Ye know, I just finished icing a Christmas cake. I baked it back in October, ye know. You two should come over for a slice."

Savannah immediately shook her head. "Oh, Granny, we're both a muddy mess. Trust me when I say you don't want us to come in your house."

"I wilna take no for an answer. I'll expect ye in ten minutes." With that, they heard her shuffling across the backyard and disappearing into her home.

Baxter turned and pointed a finger at Savannah. "See. And if you'd agreed to go out to dinner with me, we'd have plans."

"Are you kidding? You can't beat Granny's Christmas cake." She sounded perfectly serious, but there was humor shining in her eyes.

He held a hand out to her. "So will you join me for some of Granny Mary's magnificent Christmas cake?"

He was certain she would scoff at him or, at the very least, turn and walk away. She took him by surprise when she set her hand in his. Her skin was frigid, and it was all he could do not to clasp her hand between both of his. "Is that a yes?"

"I'm saying yes to Granny's offer." She looked down at her sweat pants and muddy boots. "I need to run in and change shoes, at least. See you over there in ten?" She pulled her hand away.

He hadn't even agreed before she'd disappeared through the sliding glass door. Maybe going next door for dessert wasn't what he'd planned, but he wasn't about to give up the chance to spend some extra time with her.

Besides, she was right. Granny's cake was incredible.

Ten minutes later, Granny ushered them inside her home. They both took their shoes off at the front door and followed her into the kitchen. The tiny table had three chairs crowded around it. She motioned for them to sit.

"I'll bring the cake right out. Make yerselves comfortable."

Baxter held the chair for Savannah and helped her scoot it in. As soon as he sat down, he realized just how small the table was. His knee touched Savannah's. It didn't matter how he shifted, there wasn't quite enough room under the table to maintain distance between them. Not that he particularly minded.

Savannah was looking everywhere but at him. Baxter finally nudged her knee with his own. "I won't bite, you know."

Her cheeks turned pink within moments. "Yeah."

He covered a chuckle as Granny returned, a plate of cake in each hand. She set one down in front of each of them along with a fork. "Here ya go. Would ya like a glass of milk to go with it?"

"That would be wonderful, Granny, thank you." Baxter admired his slice of cake. "This looks almost too good to eat."

Granny patted him on the shoulder. "Aren't ya sweet. Savannah? Milk?"

"Yes, please."

"I'll be right back."

Savannah took a small bite of her cake and moaned in appreciation. "I'm confident I could never produce a Christmas cake as decadent as this."

Baxter had to agree. There had only been a few times in the past he'd tasted Granny's famous Christmas cake. It was always worth it.

Granny returned with the glasses of milk and then joined them at the table. "I'm so glad ya both like it."

They talked about the Christmas season coming up, decorating for the holidays, and some of their favorite Christmas memories.

A half hour later, Baxter and Savannah thanked her for the amazing dessert and waved goodbye. He walked Savannah to the front of the Potters' house. Before she went inside, he put a hand on her arm.

"So I have a question for you."

She turned to face him. "What's that?"

"We sat down at the same table, and neither of us self-combusted." He paused for effect. "Given that evidence, is there any chance you might give me a different answer next time I ask you out to dinner?"

The corners of Savannah's mouth twitched. "You are stubborn."

"Yep." He was still touching her arm. He slid it down to her hand and took it in his. "So?"

"Ask me next time, and you'll find out." She flashed him a pretty smile. "I should probably get inside."

"Of course." He squeezed her hand before releasing it. "Thank you again for all the help on the fence. I couldn't have made so much progress without you. I think we make a good team."

"Surprisingly, so do I." Savannah unlocked the front door, stepped through the doorframe, and turned back with a smile. "Good night, Baxter."

"Good night, Savannah."

She closed the door behind her. Baxter felt the first drop of rain in the next round of showers and retreated to his car before it started to pour. Thinking about his time working on the fence with Savannah had him smiling all the way home.

After his last girlfriend, he'd sworn he wouldn't put himself in a position where a woman would make him second-guess what he wanted for his future. He'd about given up any possibility of raising a family of his own in a small town.

Then he thought about Savannah. Sure, it was early in their friendship, but he could see her happy about staying in Romance. Maybe even opening her own bakery one day. He thought about Granny and then pictured Savannah making homemade cakes for her children's birthdays. That thought made his heart stutter.

The last thing he needed to do was get ahead of himself. He hadn't even convinced the woman to go on a date with him. Yet.

Chapter Six

Baxter nailed the last fence picket in place the following Thursday evening. He tossed the hammer into the open toolbox and stood back to admire his work with satisfaction. It'd taken a little longer than he'd anticipated, but he still had one week before Christmas and at least two weeks before his grandparents returned to accomplish the rest of his to-do list.

Besides, taking longer only meant more time at the house which, in turn, meant more time with Savannah. She'd come out one other time to help with the fencing. He hadn't asked her to dinner again, although he had every intention of doing so. He just had to wait for the right time.

A high-pitched scream from the house made the hair on the back of his neck stand on end. He grabbed the hammer again on instinct and sprinted toward the sliding glass door.

With no idea what to expect, he didn't bother wiping his shoes off before opening the door and going inside. "Savannah?"

"In here!"

He followed the sound of her voice to the kitchen where she was holding several towels against the kitchen faucet. Water sprayed everywhere from the base of the faucet. Baxter wasn't sure which was wetter: the counters, the wall, or Savannah.

"What happened?"

"I was washing dishes, and the faucet exploded. I'm not sure how to turn it off." She still held the towels in place. She leaned forward and brushed her forehead against her arm to get wet tendrils of hair out of her eyes.

"Here, watch out." He knelt in front of the cabinet under the sink, and she shifted over to give him more room. Baxter found the shut-off valve and within seconds the water had stopped flowing.

"Thank you." Savannah dropped the soaked towels into the sink and sagged against the counter. "If you hadn't come in, the Potters may have come home to an indoor swimming pool."

The image had Baxter laughing. Both of the dogs wandered into the room. Nessie lapped up water while Nellie followed the muddy footprints Baxter had tracked in from the back door.

He pointed them out. "I'm afraid I only contributed to the mess."

She nodded toward the hammer on the kitchen counter. He must have set it down there when he first saw her wrestling with the faucet. "What were you going to do with that?"

Baxter exaggerated his posture by straightening his spine. "I had no idea why you screamed, and I suspect these dogs don't have a lot of bite to go with their bark."

There was humor in her eyes but also appreciation. "I'm just glad you knew how to turn that stupid faucet off. I guess I should call a plumber."

"Probably a good idea. I'd offer to help, but my skills are severely limited in that area. You call, and I'll get some towels and a mop and see if I can get a start on cleaning this up."

She nodded. After drying her hands and arms on another towel, she disappeared into the living room with both dogs on her heels.

By the time she'd returned ten minutes later, Baxter had dried off the counter and mopped up most of the floor. Savannah's quick response with the towels probably redirected most of the water back into the sink. It could've been worse.

"Okay, they can't get anyone here until Monday. But it's really not that big of a deal. I can manage for a few days without the kitchen sink." Savannah looked up from her phone. "Wow, you made fast progress. I put the dogs in the other room for now."

Baxter rested his arm on the handle of the mop. "That's good. It'll be a pain without water, though."

She shrugged. "I'm mostly using paper plates and things like that anyway. It'll be fine. And I can get water for the dogs from the bathroom."

It sounded like she had everything lined up. Baxter straightened and went to mop up the remaining water when Savannah came around the corner. She was just about to step in one of the last puddles. "Watch out—"

His caution came too late. The moment her shoe hit the water, it slid right out from under her. Baxter grabbed one of her flailing arms before she fell completely and kept her upright. "Whoa. You okay?"

Savannah's foot slipped again. She wrapped her arms around his to keep herself steady. "That sink is out to get me one way or another, isn't it?" Her long eyelashes lifted until her gaze tangled with his. Her sweet scent enveloped him, and it took everything in his power to not draw her closer. He was just now getting her to let him into her world. As much as he wanted to kiss her, it wouldn't be worth it if it caused their newfound friendship to crash down around them.

❄ ❄ ❄

Savannah's breath caught in her throat. Baxter's strong arms kept her from falling. She ought to let go and create some space between them, but the intensity in his gaze kept her rooted. His breath fanned across her cheek. For just a moment, she thought he might kiss her. In that same moment, she could hardly believe she actually wanted him to.

The realization came only a heartbeat before he loosened his grip and took a step away. The intense disappointment made no sense. After all, this was the guy she couldn't stand a couple short weeks ago. Just how pathetic was she?

She cleared her throat, crossed her arms in front of her, and took a steadying breath. "Thanks. Again. I owe you one."

His eyebrows lifted. She already knew what he would say before he spoke the words. "Go out with me. One date."

He'd just saved her twice in the span of thirty minutes. How was she supposed to say no now? "What do you have in mind?"

Baxter grinned and gave her a wink. "It's a surprise, but I promise it'll be fun. Do you have to get up early on Saturday?"

"No, I'm not working for a change."

"Great. Then how does six o'clock sound? Assuming, of course, that you can handle a later night." There was a friendly challenge in his words.

"Tomorrow, huh? Why are you in such a hurry?"

"Because I'm not about to give you time to change your mind."

Savannah tried to act nonchalant while her heart ping-ponged around in her chest. "Tomorrow night is fine." She held up a single finger. "*One* date."

The happy look on his face had her smiling in return. They went to work again and finished wiping up the rest of the water. The whole kitchen floor shined. Savannah had a feeling Mrs. Potter would be impressed if she could see it now.

"I got a call from the Potters last night. Little Sarah was taken off the ventilator yesterday. That's a huge step. She's still on extra oxygen, but they're hoping that might be decreased over the next few days as well."

"That's great news," Baxter said as he tossed the last of the wet towels into the washing machine. "Hopefully I'll get to meet that tiny cousin of mine this year. It's sad that I don't see all of them very often."

"It seems like that's the way families are anymore. Everyone's so spread out."

Baxter hesitated as though there were something he wanted to say, but he wasn't sure whether he should. "So what's kept you here in Romance?"

She thought about that a moment. "A large part of it is because of my family. It'd take a lot to make me leave my parents or Katrina and Kyle. I also haven't had a reason to. Everything I've needed is here." It sounded simple, but it was also true. She knew a lot of kids in high school whose main goal in life was to get out of Romance. Some of them did. But the thought of leaving the place where she grew up always made Savannah sad. "I've got a family that supports me, a job I've worked toward, and a great community. At some point, I'd like to get a better apartment." She laughed. "But overall, I can't complain."

"That's great. I think it's important to have a sense of belonging." Baxter slid his hands into his pockets. He seemed to search for something to say. "You know, it's a shame that my grandparents didn't decorate this place. Would you normally have a tree in your apartment?"

Savannah nodded. "I would. But I'm just considering it a break from having to unpack and pack up all the decorations." Their conversation lulled. "Do you need more help outside tonight?"

He blinked as though he'd forgotten about working out there at all. "No, thank you. I finished the fence. I think I may take off early tonight. Formulate my plan of attack for the rest of my list." He picked up the hammer. "I hope you have an uneventful rest of your day."

"Yeah, me, too." She walked him back to the door. "Thanks again for your help."

"Anytime." He tipped an imaginary hat. "I'll talk to you tomorrow."

She watched him walk out, gather the rest of his tools, and disappear through one of the side gates before she closed the door and hanging blinds.

Her head spun with all that had happened in the last couple of weeks. She'd gone from dreading that Baxter was back in town to having a date with him tomorrow night.

She could only imagine how much Katrina would tease her once she found out. Savannah might avoid telling her entirely except that, in this small town, word would spread like wildfire anyway.

Chapter Seven

Savannah took in Romance's most popular pizza parlor and smiled. "You're kidding." Of all the places she'd imagined Baxter might surprise her with dinner, this hadn't even crossed her mind.

"What? Not a pizza fan?" The look of concern on his face was sweet. "We can go somewhere else if you'd prefer."

"No, no. Pizza's great. This just wasn't what I expected." The scents of pepperoni, tomato sauce, and cheese wafted to her nose. A long growl reached her ears, and she laughed. "I think my stomach agrees that this was the perfect choice."

Baxter grinned and put a hand against her lower back as he guided her through the line. He purchased two buffets, drinks, and a whole cup full of tokens. "You can't have pizza without video games."

They found a table and filled their plates before sitting. Savannah bit into her piece of pizza and nodded approvingly. "I need to eat here more often." She caught him giving her a funny look. "What? Not a fan of macaroni and cheese pizza?"

"Not even a little. Why someone would combine the two, I'll never know." He lifted his own slice. "The craziest I get is eating sausage and pepperoni together."

Savannah took another exaggerated bite and enjoyed the way his eyes sparkled in humor.

They ate, although all the noise from the many families coming in for dinner made it difficult to hold much of a conversation. Once they'd finished, Baxter held up the cup of tokens and shook them. "You ready for some fun?"

She stood decisively. "You bet."

"Great. We have about an hour, then we need to head to part two of this evening's entertainment." When she started to ask him what he was talking about, he shook his head. "Nope, you'll find out later. Come on, let's see if they still have Rampage."

Twenty minutes later, Savannah watched Baxter as he destroyed the high scores on Pacman. "I had no idea you were so good at this."

"Oh, my buddies and I spent way too much time here when we were in school. I think it's awesome they kept most of these old games. Nothing new can compete with them." The ghosts finally caught up with him, and he stepped away from the joystick. "Your turn."

"No, thank you. I don't think I could even try to beat that kind of score. Besides, I was more of a Nintendo kid. Smash Bros., Zelda." She leaned against a nearby arcade game. "My parents, sister, and I would stay up way too late playing them and snack on way too much popcorn."

"That sounds like a lot of fun."

"It really was." She motioned to the surrounding games. "This reminds me it's something I ought to make time for again. At least once in a while." She didn't schedule enough plain fun in her life.

"I think that's important." Baxter watched her for several moments as though he were trying to read between the lines.

The guys she'd dated in the past had all been nice enough. But everything was superficial. She'd gone through the motions of going out to dinner and going on walks. As soon as it got to be more personal than that, she'd pull away. She'd never been the thin, pretty girl in high school, and she certainly didn't qualify as either now.

Katrina told her she was too self-conscious. Savannah knew she was right, but it didn't make it easy for her to change the way she felt about herself. Or the idea of letting a guy get close enough to where, if he rejected her, it'd actually hurt.

She reached out and tapped the cup that had only a few tokens left. "Come on, let's see how good you are at Skee-Ball."

The thought crossed her mind that she was having more fun on this supposed date with Baxter than she had with probably any other date she could remember. She quickly squelched it and focused on trying to toss the small, wooden balls into the numbered holes at the end of the ramp. Coming here was a great idea, and it only had her curious about what Baxter had planned next.

❄ ❄ ❄

Baxter liked this new relaxed Savannah. He'd been afraid she'd hate the idea of pizza and games, but she'd jumped right in. They combined their tickets from their poor attempts at Skee-Ball. He waited as she tried to find something to trade them in for. When she returned, she handed him a blue bouncy ball. "Your share of the winnings."

"My favorite color." He bounced it off the floor and caught it easily. "What'd you get?"

She popped a purple monster pencil topper on her index finger.

He laughed. "Now that's scary."

"She was the last one. I couldn't just leave her there alone." Savannah made the monster dance a moment before she gently patted it on the head. "Besides, they were about the only thing we could afford."

"I guess we wouldn't win any Skee-Ball awards, would we?"

"Yeah, probably not." The smile she gave Baxter convinced him he couldn't have been happier winning anything else. "So what do you say? You ready for the next installment in our evening of fun?"

She took the monster off and tucked it into her bag. "You've been doing all right so far. I'm curious to see what you've got planned next."

He'd worried before that she wouldn't find his dinner plans fancy enough. He should've known better, though. While they may not have been great friends growing up, she'd always been the no-nonsense kind of girl.

A detail among many that definitely appealed to him. He escorted her back to his car and then drove across town. He could tell she was trying to guess his destination. They had enough time, so he took several extra turns just to throw her off. He finally pulled up in front of the elegant Esmeralda Theater. The large marquee out front highlighted the movies playing this week.

Savannah chuckled. "You keep surprising me."

He parked and turned toward her. "Is that a bad thing?"

She studied his face for a moment before shaking her head. "No."

"Good." He got out and went around to open the door. "If you will come with me, I've already got tickets to tonight's showing of *White Christmas*. Did you save room for popcorn?"

"Are you kidding? There's always room for popcorn."

Yep, she was a girl after his own heart.

Marianne Carter, the owner and manager of the theater, greeted them with a happy smile. "Come on in, you two. Welcome!" Marianne often dressed to match the holiday movies she was showing. Tonight, she sported blonde curls and wore a white sparkling sweater, leggings, and shoes just like Vera-Ellen from *White Christmas*.

Savannah gave her a hug. "You look amazing."

"Thank you. It's always fun dressing up." She motioned to the concession area as another couple entered the theater. "Make yourself at home." Marianne turned to greet the newcomers.

Baxter purchased their snacks. Once they got everything and settled into their seats, they set the large tub of popcorn between them. As the lights began to dim, Baxter looked at Savannah with mock seriousness. "Now, you have seen this movie before, right?"

The lack of light made it difficult to see her face, but her giggle washed over him. "Once or twice."

"Okay, just checking. I was going to say that, if you hadn't, we need to have a serious talk about your lack of appreciation for classic Christmas movies."

The film began, and Baxter split his attention between the movie he knew by heart, and the occasional feel of Savannah's hand when his bumped into it while reaching for popcorn. Every time it happened, he had to fight the instinct to abandon the popcorn in favor of holding her hand.

He managed to stick to his plan until they were over halfway through the movie. He'd gone for another handful of popcorn. This time, their hands went into the tub at the same time, and they both stilled. Uncertain how Savannah was feeling, he softly caressed the skin on the back of her fingers with his thumb. It wasn't until she'd turned her hand a little and opened her palm that he took it in his. Their fingers naturally laced together, and that's exactly where they stayed for the remainder of the movie.

The credits began to roll, and the lights slowly came back on again. Baxter glanced at their joined hands, gave hers a squeeze, and looked at Savannah's face. She gave him a shy smile as though she were about as shocked as he was to see they really were still holding hands.

Reluctantly, he released hers and stood. "You can't go wrong with these classic Christmas movies." He picked up the tub of popcorn and offered it to Savannah. When she shook her head, he threw it out on their way to the main part of the theater.

"That was fun. Thank you, Baxter."

"You're welcome." He waited until they'd exited the building into the cool night air. "I have one more thing planned for tonight."

Savannah glanced at her watch, noted the late hour, and raised an eyebrow.

Baxter chuckled. "Oh, come on. Live a little." He gently bumped her shoulder with his. "I promise you'll like it. So, are you in? I'll have you home in an hour."

Now it was her turn to laugh. "Yes, I'm in. And if it takes longer than an hour, I'm sure I'll survive."

"I'm glad." He helped her into the passenger side before going around and getting behind the wheel. He drove through town to the other side. He'd just read about Cherry Circle in the paper. The neighborhood loop was supposed to be one of the most highly decorated neighborhoods in town. He'd heard nothing but good things about it and thought it would be a great way to end the evening.

As they neared the street, he slowed behind a line of cars. That's when he turned the radio on so that Christmas music filled the cab.

"Oh! Are we checking out Christmas on Cherry Circle?" Savannah leaned forward in her seat and tried to see around the cars in front of them. "Katrina took Kyle and said it was awesome. I was going to go last year but never got around to it."

"I thought it might be fun."

The line of cars inched forward, but it didn't matter. Between the Christmas music playing on the radio and Savannah's presence, it could take all night and Baxter would be just fine. They compared holiday decorating horror stories from their childhoods, the worst gifts they'd ever received, and then also the best ones.

"I guess my favorite gift would have to be the year my parents bought me a certificate to a baking class. I was probably thirteen." Savannah watched as the Christmas lights grew closer, her voice sounding wistful in the near darkness. "I know it sounds crazy to you, but it was like a dream come true. Especially because it meant getting some more cooking tips so my cupcakes never made you or anyone else gag again."

The humorous lilt in her voice told him she wasn't holding it against him anymore. He was glad, but he still felt bad about the whole thing. He couldn't have known his reaction had made her feel so bad. He reached for her hand again and pressed a kiss to her knuckles. "I really am sorry about that. I promise I won't ever again gag over one of your delectable pastries."

She laughed. "I appreciate that." She leaned forward in her seat. "Oh, here we go!"

The lights they'd been seeing as they drew closer were now just outside the windows. The neighborhood had gone all out, and Baxter wondered just how much electricity they'd pulled in to put up a display this elaborate.

They eventually rolled down their windows and turned the radio off because there was even music being piped into the front yards to match the different themes. As they slowly made their way through the half-circle neighborhood, he and Savannah commented on the different yards. He had to admit his favorite was the Star Wars decorations, complete with a Wookie wearing a Christmas hat. That the house was playing the song "What Do You Get a Wookie for Christmas?" only secured it at the top of the list.

"That one was pretty epic," she agreed. "Although I especially liked the winter wonderland." The front yard had looked like a snow-covered hill. There were animals building snowmen, making snow angels, and even throwing snowballs at each other. "I hope it snows for Christmas this year."

Her voice sounded wistful. Baxter wasn't particularly fond of winter weather. But right then, he was sure he'd march right up to the North Pole himself and request a snowfall for her for the holidays. "They're saying we have a chance."

"I sure hope they're right."

By the time they finished touring the neighborhood, Savannah was hiding a yawn behind her hand. He smiled a little and began the drive back to his grandparents' house. It was definitely the black sheep on the street with every other house lit up with Christmas lights, decorations, or at least the silhouette of a colorful tree visible through the window. The porch light hadn't even been turned on.

Baxter pulled into the driveway. "I'll walk you to the door. I didn't even think about the light when we left."

"Me, either."

The moment she stepped onto the driveway, Baxter offered her his arm. She slipped her hand through it and flashed him a pretty smile as he led her toward the front door.

"I had a great time, Baxter. Thank you again for insisting I go out tonight."

Her choice of words had him chuckling. "You're welcome. I think." He waited for her to open the front door. The two dogs ran to them, tails wagging, and light from inside the house flooded the porch. "I know I kept you out way past your bedtime. I promise I won't show up too early tomorrow to tackle the back deck so you can sleep in."

"I appreciate that." She lifted her chin to look into his face. What he saw in her eyes was a mixture of curiosity and nerves. Probably a good representation of what she was seeing in him.

He cupped her elbow and leaned in to place a kiss on her cheek beside the corner of her mouth. "Have a good night, Savannah. I'll see you tomorrow."

"Good night, Baxter."

She gave a little wave as she fought her way past the dogs to get inside the house. He waited until the door had closed and he heard the locks slide into place before going back to his vehicle.

When he'd first asked Savannah to go out with him tonight, there were a lot of different scenarios he'd played out in his mind. But it'd all gone better than any of them. Not to mention he should get an award for not outright kissing her underneath that porch light.

He thought about how much she enjoyed the Christmas lights and then about how less-than-cheery his grandparents' house was. That's when he got an idea that he continued to piece together well into the night.

Chapter Eight

Savannah slept in until nearly nine Saturday morning. She might have slept later, but Nessie and Nellie would have none of it. Between their need to go outside and being convinced they were starving to death, they were bound to get her out of bed one way or another.

Once the dogs were cared for, Savannah sat at the little kitchen table with a glass of orange juice and a Pop-Tart. It was rare to not be working at Sweet Hearts on a Saturday morning. That's usually where she got her breakfast that day, so the Pop-Tart was a poor substitute. Still, it was better than nothing.

She let her mind wander over the events of the previous evening. Everything about it had been perfect. And that moment on the front porch when he brought her back? She sighed. She'd never wanted to kiss a guy—and not wanted to kiss a guy—so much at the same time in her life. When his lips had caressed her cheek, she'd been both relieved and disappointed.

It left her wondering whether he'd wanted to truly kiss her, too.

She popped the last bite of her breakfast in her mouth and groaned.

If someone had told her years ago that she'd one day wish Baxter Reid would kiss her, she never would've believed it. She wasn't even sure she believed it now.

Savannah rolled her eyes at herself. It was probably just all the holiday cheer from last night. Baxter kissed her on the cheek because he thought he had to do something and wasn't about to give her a proper kiss.

A decision she was fine with. She'd convinced herself of that for a whole five minutes until she found herself watching the clock and wondering when he'd get there to work on the back porch.

The quickening of her pulse told her just how much of a liar she was.

She spent some time on her laptop and tried to ignore the clock. She'd almost succeeded when there was a knock at the door. Half expecting it to be Mom, she opened it to find Baxter standing on the porch. It was the freshly cut pine tree he had balanced beside him that surprised her the most.

Her eyes widened. "What on earth?"

Baxter grinned. "I thought it was just plain sad that one of the biggest fans of Christmas I know is spending it in a house devoid of Christmas decorations." He motioned to the tree with flair. "So I thought I'd remedy that. I brought a stand and decorations, too."

He was every bit serious as he waited for her reaction with a dash of vulnerability. It was one of the sweetest things anyone had ever done for her.

She held the screen door open wide and ushered him in. "By all means, let's give this place some Christmas cheer."

While Baxter brought in the tree stand and several boxes, Savannah found some Christmas music on her laptop and got it playing. Before long, they had the tree straightened. Baxter withdrew several strands of lights. "You strike me as a multi-color gal." He plugged the first strand into the wall and yellow, blue, red, green, pink, and orange lights immediately came to life. "Am I wrong?"

Savannah shook her head. "No, you're not wrong." She reached out to finger some of the bulbs. They were already getting warm. "They've always been my favorite."

"I thought that might be the case." He winked and then wound the lights around the tree, which turned out to be taller and more full than she originally thought. It took two of the strands to cover the tree.

When Baxter tucked the end into a branch, he stood back with satisfaction. "Yep, there we go. And we have an extra strand to put across the mantle or something if you want."

"That'll be great."

He picked up another box and deposited it at her feet. "Here, you start on the decorations, and I'll get this strand tacked up along the mantle for you."

Savannah lifted the lid off the box and dug through a variety of Christmas ornaments. Many of them looked handmade. "Where did you get all of these?"

"My mom was always big into arts and crafts, and she was particularly inspired around Christmas. Most of those are ornaments I made at some point during my childhood. When I grew up and moved out, Mom and Dad gave them all to me. I can't possibly fit them all on my own tree, so I thought I'd share."

She tried to picture Baxter working on a pinecone reindeer or painting a wooden Santa ornament and just couldn't quite do it. She hung both up on the tree along with several glittering stars and a small foil bell with a jingle bell in the center. The next thing she found had her fighting back the laughter. She finally held it up for Baxter to see. "Okay, explain this one."

Baxter secured part of the lights before looking up. The moment he did, his ears grew red. He walked up to her and took the ornament. "Yeah, well. I was probably seven or eight. Mom wanted us to paint these wooden reindeer and then glue them to the platform. We then added snow and white glitter."

Which had since fallen off, apparently. Savannah couldn't contain her grin. "And these black beads underneath the reindeer?"

"Yeah. Well, even Santa's reindeer have to poop sometime, right?"

Her laughter took over then.

He rubbed one of his ears that had only gotten more red as he joined her. "I don't even know what to say. I think I did it just to get a rise out of Mom. But she kept it anyway." He held the ornament in front of him with a shake of his head. "I forgot I still had it. Here, we'll just toss it in the empty box for me to take back."

"Oh, no, we won't." Savannah swiped the ornament from his hand. "It deserves a prominent spot on this tree, poop and all." She hung it with a flourish. "There, see? It'll make me think of you every time I see it."

"Perfect," he said, the word laced with sarcasm. "I'll make a mental note to toss it when we take down the tree."

"Don't you dare." She placed her hands on her hips. "One day, your little boy will do something similar, and you'll wish you'd kept it to show him.

Maybe making a reindeer poop in the snow will become a Reid family tradition."

The look on his face slowly shifted to a more serious expression. It looked as though he were about to ask her something when he quickly diverted his attention back to the box. The smile on his face returned. "I'd better go through the rest of these and make sure nothing else embarrassing slipped through the cracks…"

❊   ❊   ❊

Baxter didn't know if Savannah would love his surprise the moment he thought of it the night before. Helping her decorate the living room and make it more Christmassy was a lot more fun than sanding and re-staining the back deck. Besides, he still had plenty of time to get that done before his grandparents returned.

He knew he'd enjoy decorating the tree, but he hadn't expected the whole thing to feel so… domestic. He'd already been wondering what it would be like to decorate a house together one day. Their house.

Then she had to go and mention him having a son. And the first thing that went through his mind? That he would be "their son." The thought had come from nowhere and made him realize just how quickly he was falling for Savannah. He'd liked her for as long as he could remember, but there'd always been a distance between them. Only lately had he understood how much of that was his responsibility.

Now she was opening up to him. Laughing with him. He loved every minute of it. He could easily see himself coming home to this every evening. The thought both terrified and intrigued him.

He quickly finished the lights across the mantle and then helped Savannah finish decorating the tree. He retrieved the last box. "Okay, so I was trying to think of a topper for the tree, and I didn't have much luck until I found this."

He pulled out an item wrapped in tissue paper. It was only partially unwrapped when he heard Savannah gasp.

"You actually kept that?"

He held the large golden star for her to see. "I did."

It'd been one of the last Christmases he'd seen Savannah. He was thinking they were both fourteen. Grandma had wanted to do a gift exchange using a game. People drew numbers, got a gift that someone else brought, and could choose to keep it or exchange it for a different one.

He'd heard Savannah telling someone in the living room about how she'd found the star tree topper, repainted it, and then added some glitter to make it sparkle. The star was beautiful in its simplicity.

Savannah reached out and touched it. "You know, I was mortified when you traded your bag of Christmas M&Ms for that star. At the time, I thought you were the worst person to end up with it. I guess I just figured you went home and shot at it with your slingshot or something."

"I thought about it." He gave her a teasing wink. "Honestly, I thought you'd done a great job. My parents had just started talking about moving a couple of weeks before, and I decided I wanted to keep it to remember you by. Later they chose to wait until I'd graduated from high school." He shrugged. "I bet you never would've guessed I was the sentimental type."

"Not in a million years."

"Of course, I wasn't that way about everyone." He gathered some hair that was framing her face and carefully tucked it behind one ear. "Only a particular girl that I kinda had a crush on back in the day."

Her chin lifted, and she looked at him incredulously. "No way."

"Obviously I wasn't real good at showing it. Seeing as I somehow drove her to hate me." He smiled at her and carefully placed the star on the top of the tree. "See, it looks perfect up there. Don't you think?"

"It does look great." She laid a hand on his arm, bringing his attention to her face. "I never hated you. Well, not really. I don't hate you now."

"I'm glad." He covered her hand with his. It was weird how his heart rate had picked up like a racing train while his breathing had slowed. The way she was looking at him now was something he never wanted to forget.

"There's one more thing I did in our youth that I should probably set right." It was hard walking away from her long enough to go back to that box. He'd put this last thing in the bottom because he hadn't been sure whether he'd take it out at all or not. "There was one Christmas where I was being a real jerk. I hung a piece of mistletoe above a doorframe. Do you remember that?"

Savannah's cheeks immediately turned pink, and her eyes flashed. "I refused to walk under it, and so you pushed me until I did."

Baxter winced. "Not one of my finest moments. I didn't expect Joe to swoop in and kiss you."

She stuck her tongue out and made a face. "Yeah, that was pretty awful. For the record, I wanted to smack you with something that day."

"I would've deserved it." He hesitated, his hand still on the item in the box. "I was an idiot, Savannah. Because I'd never been so jealous of anyone until that moment when Joe kissed you."

Her mouth opened in surprise and closed again. Her eyes had widened as she stared at him, clearly unsure of what to say.

"So I thought it was only right to set the record straight." He lifted a bunch of mistletoe out of the box and held it up in front of him. "I won't push you to stand under it. And I checked the front door to make sure it was locked so Joe couldn't come storming in."

That last part had Savannah chuckling. She ran a hand down the side of her face before fiddling with the hem of her shirt. He liked that she seemed every bit as nervous as he felt right then.

He tied a small string to the mistletoe and hung it in the same doorway he had many years ago. "I don't know if things would've been different between us if I'd been the one to kiss you back then. Maybe you would've hated me more." He shrugged. "But I do know I was severely disappointed I didn't kiss you that day."

"I'd had no idea," she said, just above a whisper.

Baxter held a hand out to her. "What do you say? Give this poor guy a chance to fix a past mistake?"

He waited, his heart hammering in his ears. When Savannah placed her hand in his, it took nearly everything he had to not whoop with joy. He guided them under the mistletoe together, cupped her cheek, and leaned in until his lips covered hers.

He'd had his fair share of kisses, but this was different. When she sighed and leaned into him, he put an arm around her and deepened their kiss. He wanted her to know he cared about her. That this was more than just a random kiss under the mistletoe. This was what he hoped was the start of something real between them.

When he broke the kiss, he placed another smaller one on her cheek and leaned back, his hand still threaded in her hair at the base of her neck. He gave her a small smile, enjoying the dazed look on her face.

A rustling sound drew both their attentions to the dogs, who were busy sticking their heads in that last box and rustling around in it. He and Savannah both laughed.

Baxter dropped his hand, their spell broken. "I'd better get that cleaned up. There are mistletoe leaves in there, and I don't know if it's okay for a dog to eat them."

Together, he and Savannah put lids on the boxes and then he carried them back out to the car. When he reentered the house, he nodded approvingly at the way the tree and the lights above the mantle changed the entire feel of the room. "This looks a lot better now."

Savannah reached out one hand and touched a bough on the tree. "It's perfect. Thank you, Baxter."

"You're welcome." He thought about kissing her again but knew if he did, he'd never get outside. "I'd better get out and work on the deck for a while. It's cold today; you should stay in here and enjoy the lights and stay warm." He reached out and touched her arm. "I'll check in again when I finish."

"Okay."

He carried a mental image of her sweet smile with him as he went to retrieve his tools and supplies.

Chapter Nine

Monday morning, Baxter couldn't stop whistling Christmas tunes and smiling to himself. The weekend with Savannah had been amazing. After he'd finished working on the deck, he'd taken her out for dinner, and they'd talked for a while. When he dropped her off at the house again, they'd kissed, and it was even better than the first time. He was certain kissing Savannah was on the top of his list of favorite things to do.

He didn't see her yesterday. Now he was looking forward to finishing the workday so he could drop by and put the stain on the deck this evening and visit with her then.

He pictured her at Sweet Hearts right now, creating pastry masterpieces, and smiled.

His cousin tapped on his office door. "Hey, Baxter. We've got a customer who'd like to go over some future business changes. Do you have time?"

"Sure. Send him in." Baxter cleared the loose papers from his desk and deposited them in a drawer before turning the lock on it. When he looked up, he recognized the man but couldn't quite place him. He stood. "Baxter Reid."

"Jay Warren." The man shook his hand and then took the chair offered to him. He produced an accordion folder that he promptly opened. "I own a pastry shop in town. Recently, I've had an investor interested in helping me open two or three more. If that goes well, we may turn Sweet Hearts into a chain."

Baxter nodded as he took the business proposal and leafed through it. He wondered if Savannah knew anything about this. Everything in the business plan seemed sound. Baxter pointed out a few loose ends, and Jay seemed happy to either explain them or acknowledge they were something he should think about.

Baxter tapped the cover of the proposal. "So I'm not seeing any timeline here. What are you thinking?"

"I'd like to open the first new location in Portland around Easter, and if that goes smoothly, possibly a second one on the other side of town there. Then maybe expand to include one in Salem, another in the Eugene area." He shrugged. "I'm trying not to get too far ahead of myself yet. I haven't even mentioned it to my employees, although I was thinking about doing that this week. I just wanted to run these ideas by someone else first."

"I imagine things are too busy this time of the year to focus on the other stores yet."

"Exactly. My hope is to have my baker, Savannah, go to each of the three new locations and train someone. Even though I'll have several stores, we want everything baked fresh each morning. That's where she comes in: to make sure whatever bakers we hire carry on the same recipes and quality pastries customers in Romance are used to finding at Sweet Hearts."

Baxter fought to maintain a neutral expression. "So you're hoping she'll train and manage each of the bakeries at first?"

Jay nodded. "I know it'll be a lot of work. But once all three or four are open, it's my hope she can help me rotate between the four stores to make sure they're being run the way I want them to be. Who knows? If it's successful enough, we may continue to expand. Eventually, I hope to offer one of the stores to Savannah for her to manage. Maybe even own someday, if that's something she's interested in."

Baxter's mind tangled with the different scenarios. Even if everything went off without a hitch at each store, it would mean Savannah traveling and working long hours for several years. She'd talked about owning her own bakery for as long as he'd known her. There's no way she'd turn this opportunity down. And she shouldn't.

But the thought of having her travel all over Oregon made him feel sick. If Jay decided to expand his business to other states, would he send Savannah there to train people as well? He knew she'd mostly stuck around Romance until now. She might find she preferred to travel once she got a taste of it.

He tried to focus on the man sitting in front of him. "It sounds like you've got everything pretty much in place. Are there any figures you want to go over?"

"I did have some questions about…"

It took everything Baxter had to continue to help Jay. Two hours later, they shook hands, and Baxter walked him to the door of the credit union. This time, when he went back to his office, whistling Christmas tunes was about the last thing he felt like doing.

Here he'd thought the timing was right between him and Savannah. That maybe he'd finally found the right woman to spend the rest of his life with. It figured life would throw him another curveball. What was it with him falling for women who ended up wanting to travel? Was it so wrong of him to prefer to settle down in Romance? Raise a family here?

Disappointment took residence in his chest and drove Baxter to his chair. Owning a bakery was something he knew Savannah had always wanted. This would be a dream come true for her. Jay mentioned that he would tell her about his plans sometime this week. Baxter imagined the surprise and joy on her face when he offered her the opportunity of a lifetime.

He wasn't about to stand in her way, but that didn't mean it didn't hurt to know he would lose Savannah. Especially when he'd only just begun to understand how much he truly wanted her in his life.

❄   ❄   ❄

Savannah hung up her cell phone with a frown. It was Wednesday, and this was the third day in a row that Baxter had let her know he wouldn't be by to work on the deck. She got that things might be a little crazy at work or something the first day or two. But she had a hard time believing the credit union was that busy this close to Christmas. She wondered if he was avoiding her but immediately set the thought aside. Surely not, especially after he'd worked so hard at getting her to go out with him.

She replayed the weekend's events in her mind and allowed a smile to take over. The way he'd kissed her under the mistletoe had been one of the sweetest, most romantic things she'd ever experienced. She still had to shake her head at the realization Baxter had wanted to kiss her so many years ago. She'd truly had no idea.

Honestly, she was sure she would've shoved him had he tried back then. The thought made her laugh. So maybe it was a good thing that their first kiss had come years later. Still, she wondered where they would be now if all of this had started sooner.

Maybe she wouldn't have gone through so many relationships that had only made her self-conscious and hesitant. Or maybe things would've ended badly between them back then, and she'd be right where she was now. There was no sense in playing the what-if game.

She tried to pull her focus back to the customers she was helping at Sweet Hearts. She'd already caught herself making a mistake twice because she was so preoccupied with her own thoughts.

Just before it was time for her to call it a day, Jay asked if she'd come to the back office for a few minutes. He'd mentioned maybe opening other stores in the past, but she hadn't realized how serious he was until he shared his future plans for the Sweet Hearts name. She was still trying to process everything he'd told her when she waved to her coworkers and headed out for the day.

Jay wanted to turn Sweet Hearts into a franchise. And he wanted her to train the bakers at each location? The fact he was willing to give her a choice of the new locations to manage and eventually buy was huge. She'd always dreamed of having her own bakery. And here she had the opportunity to build one from the ground up.

But it would require moving out of Romance. Just thinking about that was scary. She'd lived here all of her life. Leaving it behind—even if it was only for another town in Oregon—hurt in more ways than one. At the same time, she'd only be moving around for a few years at most. And it's not like even Salem was too far away to not be able to regularly visit her family.

What about Baxter? If this opportunity had come up even just a few weeks ago, she'd jump at the chance. Or at least seriously think about it. But now? She had no idea where she and Baxter stood. Was it too soon to define their relationship?

She didn't want to call him while he was still at work. Instead, she texted him with a brief message. "Hey! Are you coming by this evening? I wanted to talk to you about something."

Minutes later, she received his response, "Yeah, I'll be there around six to stain the deck."

That meant he'd probably eat before he arrived. Savannah had already decided to dress appropriately and go out and help. If they could get that staining done, then maybe they could spend a little time together over the weekend before Christmas. Baxter had once mentioned going to the live production of *A Christmas Carol.*

By the time Baxter arrived, Savannah was waiting for him on the back porch. She smiled brightly when he came through the gate. "Hey, stranger. Seems like forever since Sunday, doesn't it?"

"It sure does." He gave her a smile in return. He had a paint can in one hand and a bag full of brushes and other supplies in the other. He leaned in and placed a kiss on her cheek. "I'm hoping to get this all stained tonight."

Savannah held her arms out. "I'm ready to help. Just hand me a paintbrush, and I'm good to go."

"Awesome. We should have no trouble getting it finished then."

There was something about him that seemed different. She watched as he emptied the plastic bag, shook the paint can before carefully opening it, and finally handed her a brush. Instead of his normal teasing, he simply explained how to stain the boards, and they got to work.

He was probably stressed about finishing everything before the end of the year. With the weekend and then Christmas Eve and Christmas Day coming up, the month would come to a close before they knew it. Besides, if he hadn't been by this week, he'd been working a lot. The poor guy was likely just tired.

"How's everything at the credit union?" she asked as she dipped her paintbrush into the stain.

"We're trying to tie things up this week. We'll be closed for three days for Christmas. It'll be nice, I think. My cousin is practically prancing around the place like a kid on Christmas Eve." He chuckled a little before glancing at her. "How about you? I imagine it's crazy busy at Sweet Hearts this week."

"It is. But Jay's always been good about putting deadlines on orders received. We're right on track and should have three days off as well." She paused. "Jay surprised me today, though. Apparently he's looking at adding more stores in Portland, Salem, and maybe Eugene and eventually turning Sweet Hearts into a franchise. He'd talked about it for a while, but I had no idea how soon he'd planned to begin."

"Oh?" Baxter focused intently on bringing new life to the deck.

Savannah stopped working and watched for his reaction. "He said he wants me to go to the different locations and train the bakery staff. He's offering to pay the cost of wherever I live as an incentive since there'll be a lot of moving around for a while. I figure, if I can save up all the money I'm not spending on rent, maybe at the end of it all I could afford to buy one of the stores from him. I've always wanted to run my own bakery…"

Baxter stilled and looked up at her. "I think that sounds like a once-in-a-lifetime opportunity, Savannah." He smiled, but it didn't quite reach his eyes.

"You should go for it. Not many people get a chance to make their dreams come true."

"I'm not sure about the timing, though. You just moved back, and everything with us is still really new… I don't know."

Baxter rested his paintbrush on the plastic bag. "Savannah? If there's one thing I've learned, it's that you need to grab onto something you want. If you wait too long, it could very well slip through your fingers." He gave her a sad smile before returning to the deck.

What was going on with him? It wasn't like she was planning on moving away forever. It'd be months before Jay would have things progressing enough to change things for Savannah. A feeling of dread gathered in her stomach like a bowling ball. "Baxter? Are you still up for going to see *A Christmas Carol?*"

"I should probably go check on my parents this weekend. Take their gifts and everything. They mentioned they may do Christmas there on Sunday." He paused. "I'll try to get back on Christmas Eve if I can."

Disappointment warred with the dread. She totally understood about wanting to go back and spend Christmas with his family. He should do that, but he hadn't said a thing about it to her until now. She picked at the wooden handle of her brush. "My parents are hosting Christmas Eve at their house this year. It's at five if you'd like to join us. You don't need to bring anything. Believe me, we've got the menu covered. I think several of the neighbors are joining us." She held her breath, hoping he'd agree to be there.

Baxter only shook his head. "I'm not sure, Savannah. I'll just have to see how the weekend goes." He nodded toward her paintbrush. "We'd better focus so we can get this done before eight. I'll come back tomorrow and finish the front deck and will probably call that good. Once it warms up a little in late spring, I'll check with Grandpa and see what else I can help him with."

"Sure." Savannah got back to staining the deck, but her heart may as well have fallen through one of the slats into the darkness below. Baxter had just told her that if you wanted something, you had to grab onto it. She could only assume his obvious pulling away this week meant he'd changed his mind about them. For whatever reason, he didn't want her bad enough.

Her heart pinched, and tears filled her eyes. She'd opened herself up to the possibility of something with Baxter when she should've known better. She tried to focus on the deck, more than ready to escape to the emptiness of the Potters' house.

Chapter Ten

The weekend before Christmas was supposed to be fun. Instead, Savannah felt as though she were going through the motions. She did go to the play with Mom and Dad. It was awesome, and all the people who put so much work into putting it together did a fabulous job. Granny Mary directed it with style as always. But it just wasn't the same without Baxter. The entire time, she kept replaying their conversation in her head. Was there something she should've said differently? Had she missed a cue somewhere along the way that might've prepared her for what was happening now? She only wished she knew.

Now it was Christmas Eve. Savannah stared at the countertop as she held her phone to her ear.

"You haven't heard from him at all?" Katrina asked in disbelief.

"Not a word. He came by and finished the front deck at some point last week while I was at work. He was gone before I got home." Savannah sighed. "It's like he was a ghost that just appeared one day and then disappeared the next." A ghost who'd managed to worm his way into her heart. "Was this all a game? Find the girl who used to hate him and see if he could get her to change her mind?" Even she was surprised by the sarcasm and resentment that dripped from her words. She sighed. "I wish I knew what I did wrong."

"I don't think you did anything wrong, Savannah. Whatever happened was all him, or at least partially him. It really doesn't make any sense. I know you were looking forward to bringing him to Mom and Dad's house tonight. Are you still coming?"

"Are you kidding? I wouldn't miss it for the world." Savannah forced herself to smile even if her sister couldn't really see it. "I've got cookies baking in the oven as we speak." She glanced at the timer and noted that she had only a few minutes left. That would finish up the chocolate chip cookie batter. Next would be apricot.

"Oh! Did you hear?" Katrina's voice rose in excitement. "They're saying we should get snow today."

"Really?" Savannah sat up straighter and glanced at the clock. It was almost eleven in the morning. "Oh, I hope so!" See? This only proved that she needed to dig herself out of her pity party and focus on the fact that it's Christmas. She enjoyed the holiday before Baxter came back to Romance. He might have made her crazy over this last week, but she wasn't about to let him take Christmas from her, too.

A whine at the back door had her up and looking around the corner to find Nellie staring at the yard, her nose pressed against the glass. "Hold on, I need to let the dogs out real fast."

The moment she opened the sliding glass door, Nessie magically appeared from somewhere else in the house. Both dogs ran across the newly stained porch and into the grass to do their thing.

Savannah swallowed hard. Everything reminded her of Baxter now. Working on the porch together. Even the fact she could now go back to sitting in the kitchen and not have to worry about the dogs escaping through a hole in the fence.

"You still there, Savannah?"

Katrina's voice pulled Savannah from her thoughts. "Yeah, I'm here. Is it silly to hope for enough snow that we get stuck at Mom and Dad's house?" Since it was only next door, she could easily walk over to take care of the dogs. The extra work would be worth it for enough snow to cushion them from the rest of the world.

Suddenly something dawned on her. "Oh no! Is Don going to be able to make it today? When is he supposed to get into Portland?" Her brother-in-law normally got home for the weekend but had opted to work Saturday and Sunday so he could be home for Christmas Eve and Christmas Day with his family. If it snowed, driving into Romance could be a problem. It didn't snow frequently enough around there for people to really know what they're supposed to do with it. In general, snow meant the majority of the town shut down until it melted again.

"His plane is supposed to land just after two. He said he was going to try to be at Mom and Dad's in time for dinner." There was a little doubt in her voice. "Kyle's so stoked about having him home."

"He'll get here, Katrina. You'll see." The oven timer went off. She pulled the pan out and closed the oven door again. "I'd better go and mix up the next batch of cookies. I'll see you in a few hours."

"Okay. Hang in there, huh?"

"I will, you too." She ended the call and slid her phone onto the counter. Twenty minutes later, she'd mixed up the newest batch of cookies and had a pan of them baking in the oven.

It was only then that she realized she'd left the dogs outside for so long. Poor things, they were probably freezing.

She expected to find them staring through the glass waiting for her, but there was no sign of their furry bodies. They didn't come when she opened the door, either.

Savannah stepped onto the deck. "Nellie! Nessie! Come on, girls." She whistled and patted her leg. Nothing. Her stomach turned as she rushed inside to pull on some shoes. As soon as she stepped into the yard, she noticed that one of the side gates was partially open.

"No, no, no!" How did that happen? She never used the side gate. Because of that, she never would've thought to check if it'd been latched securely. She ran around the side of the house, through the gate, calling the dogs' names as she went.

"Savannah?" Mom was standing on the front porch. "Honey, what's wrong?"

"The gate came open, and the dogs ran out." Savannah put her hands on her head and tried to think. "They might've gotten out a half hour ago. Maybe even longer. I had no idea." Frustration welled up inside her. At herself. At the stupid gate. Even at the annoying canines that couldn't be content with their own backyard. "I have to find them. I won't lose the Potters' dogs on Christmas Eve." Mrs. Potter, especially, would be just devastated. "I'll go looking for them. Will you keep an eye out? If you see them come back, call me, okay?"

"I will. Your dad ran to the store. I'll call him and have him watch for them on his way home, too."

"Thanks!" She waved over her shoulder. Inside, she turned the oven off and pulled the half-baked cookies out so they wouldn't burn. After throwing on a coat, scarf, and grabbing mittens off the side table, she put the dogs' leashes in her pocket and set out to comb the street for them.

An hour in, there was no sign of the furballs. A single snowflake drifted down to land on Savannah's nose. Just perfect. The snow she so desperately wanted was going to make finding the dogs even harder, not to mention the night colder if they were stuck outside somewhere.

"Come on, you guys. Where did you go?"

❄ ❄ ❄

Baxter enjoyed the early Christmas celebration with his parents and most of his siblings. There'd been great food, gifts, and lots of laughs. There were several times he'd even managed to forget about Romance and Savannah for a while.

Okay, for a very short period of time, and it'd only happened once. Then everything came crashing back. The truth was, he missed Savannah like crazy. He missed her laugh and the way she always smelled like vanilla. He missed the way she felt in his arms.

He thought he'd hidden it all well until Dad had confronted him about it earlier that morning. They'd been sitting on the front porch in the crisp air sipping cups of coffee.

Dad looked over at Baxter. "Who put the bee in your bonnet?"

The phrase would've had Baxter laughing in his coffee if he was in a better mood. "Do you ever wonder why some things can't just come easily?"

"Sometimes." Dad was silent for several moments. "You know, they say anything worth having is worth fighting for. I really think that's true. After all, if it came too easily, then we might not appreciate it as much."

Those words kept replaying themselves in Baxter's mind all morning. When he finally announced that he'd decided to head back to Romance for the rest of Christmas Eve and Christmas, none of his family had seemed surprised, least of all Dad.

Now Baxter was driving down the highway with the windshield wipers going to keep the steady snowfall from obscuring his view of the road. He'd heard on the radio they were getting snow in Romance, too. He imagined Savannah's smile once she saw it for herself. A white Christmas was exactly what she'd been hoping for.

The unfairness of it all washed over him for the hundredth time. Why did he keep falling for women that ended up leaving and traveling the world? Or maybe he should wonder what it was about *him* that attracted them in the first place. Was there something about him that made it easy for them to leave?

With his last girlfriend, he'd simply let her go. It'd been hard, but he'd never second-guessed his decision. Not like he was doing now with Savannah. The truth was, he'd never considered fighting then.

Savannah was different. As he drove, he weighed the pros and cons of their situation. It didn't take long to realize that, as much as he hated the idea of her traveling during the week, at least she was staying in Oregon. Worst-case scenario, he'd drive to see her at the end of every week, and they'd spend the majority of the weekend together. No, it wouldn't be easy. But for her, it would be worth it. They could make it work. He could make it work.

Assuming, of course, that he hadn't messed everything up when he started to pull away. It'd been a miracle that she'd given him a second chance at all. Had he already ruined that?

The drive to Romance felt like an eternity. By the time he got into town around three, there was enough snow on the ground to make the streets slippery. It was difficult to discern where the grass and pavement began and ended.

With his heart in his throat, Baxter pulled to a stop in front of his grandparents' house, relieved to see that Savannah's car was still in the driveway. He knocked on the door several times. When no one answered, he walked next door to her parents' place.

Mrs. Miller answered with a worried look on her face. "Oh, Baxter. I didn't expect to see you. I was hoping it was Savannah."

"She isn't here?"

Mrs. Miller shook her head. "No. The dogs got out through the gate, and she's been wandering around the neighborhood trying to find them for the last couple of hours. I told her she needed to get home and warm up for a while, but she's so worried about those dogs."

"Don't worry, Mrs. Miller. I'll go see if I can find her and help out."

"I appreciate it. Tell her to call me and update me when she can, okay?"

"I will." He waved as he jogged back to his vehicle and started driving up and down the streets of the neighborhood. He finally spotted Savannah several blocks over. She had her hands to her mouth, and he could barely hear her calling the dogs' names as she walked.

He pulled up beside her on the street, reached across the cab, and opened the passenger door. "Are you crazy, woman? You're going to freeze out there."

"I've got to find these blasted dogs, Baxter."

"I know you do. And we will. But we'll search while you're getting warmed up for a while." He waved her in.

She only hesitated a moment before she climbed in and closed the door behind her. Baxter took in her red cheeks and nose and knew she had to be miserable. He turned the heater on full blast then took her hands in his, removed the gloves, and winced at how cold and red they were. "Here, hold them over the heater vents for a few minutes."

Savannah complied. "I really need to get back out there."

"And we'll roll the windows down and keep looking after you warm up a little."

She shot him a look that dared him to boss her around again. "What are you doing back? I didn't figure I'd see you again for another eight years."

Yeah, he deserved that. "I did kinda pull a disappearing act, didn't I?"

"Yep." She rubbed her hands together and put them back in front of the vents. That one word spoke of the hurt and confusion she felt. He more than understood where she was coming from.

"Look, I came back to Romance hoping to make it my home again. Eventually meet someone and raise a family here." He swallowed hard. It wasn't easy to just put it all out on the table for her. "I thought I might have found that when we reconnected." Her gaze swung to his and gave him the courage he needed to continue. "Then, when I found out you were going to take that job and be moving all the time… I guess I started wondering whether I'd been fooling myself. I know I seem like a rock-solid kind of guy, but I freaked out, Savannah."

She stared at him as though she weren't sure what to think. "Why didn't you say something? You never even gave me a chance to think about Jay's offer. If you had, you'd have found out I turned it down."

Chapter Eleven

Baxter tried to process what Savannah had just told him. She'd turned down Jay's offer? "Why would you do that?" He turned in his seat so he could see her face more clearly. "This is your dream. You can't just walk away from it."

"My dream is to open my own bakery one day." She paused. "Here in Romance. This is my home, Baxter. I never intended to live anywhere else."

He'd never considered that option. He'd just assumed she'd move to wherever the opportunity might be. He'd always had respect for her, but it just jumped up a notch. That she wasn't willing to sacrifice even the details of her dream showed a lot of integrity. "I admire that." Her hands didn't seem as red, so he pulled away from the curb and slowly made his way down the street in search of the dogs.

"Thank you." She tipped her head. "Besides, I talked to Jay. He agreed it made more sense for him to do the training, anyway. I'll manage the store here in Romance. If everything goes well with the others, Jay said I might have the opportunity to buy it." She shrugged. "Besides, I'm happy where I am right now, either way."

She rolled down her window and leaned out as she called the dogs' names.

Baxter tried to wrap his mind around everything she'd told his as they toured the neighborhood. Large, fluffy snowflakes drifted through the windows to cover the armrest and their jackets.

Savannah's phone rang, and she answered it immediately. "Hey, Dad. Any luck?" Her face brightened. "Really? Okay, yeah. We'll head that way now." She ended the call. "Someone told Dad they saw two dogs that matched Nessie's and Nellie's descriptions running near the town square."

"Awesome. Let's go." He used the controls near him to roll their windows up and headed for the center of town. The place was a bustle of activity with people strolling in the snow, Christmas lights twinkling, and big red bows peeking out from underneath a layer of glittering white.

Scott and Main Street were both lined with cars as guests gathered for Chase Lockhart and Izzy Sutton's wedding. Izzy was well-loved in Romance and ran the Interlude Inn just down the street. The extra traffic made it a little more difficult for Baxter to make his way around the square.

He was just starting to think Savannah's dad was mistaken when they spotted the dogs. There, amidst a group of children, were Nessie and Nellie having the time of their lives. Savannah laughed and leaned her head against the seat. "I ought to be furious with them right now, but I'm more relieved than anything." One boy threw a snowball, and Nellie caught it out of the air in her mouth before spitting it back out on the ground. Her antics had Savannah laughing even harder.

He turned the engine off and met her in front of the vehicle. "Let's get these dogs back to the house before they go off on another adventure."

They each lifted a dog into their arms, carried them to the truck, and got them back to his grandparents' house. Savannah let everyone know the dogs had been found. The moment the furry trouble-makers made it into the warm interior, they curled up on the carpet in the living room and went to sleep.

Savannah shook her head in mock disgust. "Just wait until I tell the Potters what you two did." Nellie's ear twitched once. Savannah turned to Baxter. "Thank you for helping me find them."

"You're welcome." He scratched the back of his neck. "I'm sorry about the other day."

"It's okay. I'm sorry, too. For assuming you'd just skipped town again. I guess jumping to conclusions is something we both did a lot of this week, isn't it?"

They shed their coats and washed up in the kitchen. Savannah placed chocolate chip cookies in a colorful tin, and Baxter quickly moved to help. She told him about the apricot cookies, and he made her promise to bake some for him to try another time.

When they'd finished cleaning up the kitchen, he reached for her hand and turned her to face him. "So, in the interest of making sure we're on the same page... I'm staying in Romance."

She tried to suppress a little smile. "And I'm staying in Romance."

"You no longer hate my guts."

Savannah laughed. "And you no longer hate my cooking."

"Nope." He snatched a cookie from the tin and popped it into his mouth. "Quite the opposite, in fact."

"Then we're good," she said, her voice soft.

"We're good." He nodded toward the mistletoe that she'd left hanging from the doorframe. "What do you say? I hate for the poor thing to only have one kiss to its name all Christmas."

Savannah wrinkled her nose. "Nah. We don't need mistletoe." She stood on her tiptoes and pressed a kiss to his cheek. Before she could move away, he caught her around the waist with one arm and pulled her closer for a proper kiss.

It didn't last nearly long enough before she put a hand on his chest. "We'd better go next door. They'll be wondering where we are."

"So I'm still invited?"

"If you can behave yourself."

"That's something I never promise." He gave her a playful wink.

❄ ❄ ❄

When Savannah walked through her parents' front door, hand in hand with Baxter, she earned several surprised looks from some of the guests. Her parents only nodded approvingly, and it was Katrina's "Well, it's about time" that had everyone laughing.

The delicious aromas of turkey and ham filled the air while Christmas carols played on the stereo system in the living room. Compared to the frigid air outside, everything about the house felt warm and cozy.

Savannah scanned the room until her gaze rested on Kyle intently watching through the front window. She lowered her voice for Katrina. "Have you heard from Don?"

"Not since he landed in Portland." She watched her son with worry. "He so wanted his dad to be here today. So did I. But the way all that snow's coming down... I'm just trying not to worry."

Savannah put an arm around her sister's shoulders. "He'll be okay."

"Yeah, I know. I need to keep us busy, though. So now that everyone else is here, what do you all say we eat?"

Kyle reluctantly came away from the window at the mention of food.

Dad held up his hand. "I'd like to say a blessing over the food, if I may." Everyone nodded in agreement and then bowed their heads. "Heavenly Father, we thank you for the many blessings you've brought to our family over the last year and the promise of new adventures that await. We thank you for the gift of your son, Jesus. And we ask that you continue to be with Don as he makes his way home."

As everyone chorused an "Amen," a cold wind blew through the living room.

They all turned to find Don standing in the doorway, snow on his coat and a smile on his face. "Amen."

"Dad!" Kyle raced through the room and into his dad's arms. "I knew you'd make it!"

Don hugged his son and then gave Katrina a thorough kiss before he shed his coat and joined the rest of the family. He glanced down at Savannah and Baxter's joined hands. "When did this happen?"

Savannah blushed as Baxter drew her close. He smiled at her in a way that sent warmth all the way down to her toes. "Let's just say Christmas is a season of miracles."

"Hear, hear," Dad said as he looked around the room at his family. "And I, for one, count the meal in that list of miracles. Come on, gang, let's eat before Kyle over there starts wasting away."

"Grandpa," Kyle objected, even though he was still the first to sit at the table.

Savannah enjoyed every moment of the meal. The food was good, but having everyone she cared about at the table with her made all the difference in the world. When they'd all stuffed themselves silly, everyone jumped into helping clean the kitchen before collapsing in chairs in the living room to visit.

Baxter caught Savannah's hand and gently tugged her away from the noisy crowd to the Christmas tree. "I bought you a present." The moment she tried to object, he put a finger to her lips. He reached into his pocket, pulled out a black velvet bag tied with a red ribbon, and laid it in her hand.

"You didn't need to get me anything." Even as she said the words, curiosity had her fingering the ribbon. It pulled open easily. She carefully tipped the bag over, emptying the contents into her palm.

A simple silver bracelet glittered in the lights from the Christmas tree. Attached to it were two charms. One was a tiny set of measuring spoons, and the other a cupcake complete with frosting and a cherry on top.

"Oh, Baxter, it's perfect."

He grinned as he helped her with the clasp. The bracelet fit her wrist perfectly. "There's plenty of room for more charms."

"This is such a sweet and thoughtful gift." She couldn't believe how detailed the little charms were. "The cupcake is a good addition."

Baxter chuckled. "Yeah, I thought so, too." His face grew serious as he softly touched her cheek with his hand. "I'm so in love with you, Savannah."

She reached up and covered his hand with her own. "I love you, too."

This time, when he kissed her, it was full of promise. In that moment, Savannah knew this would be the first of many Christmases in his arms.

SIX SWEET NOVELLAS SURE TO WARM YOUR HEART
AVAILABLE ON AMAZON

Celebrate Christmas in Romance

Welcome to Romance — an Oregon town where love lingers around every corner and residents pull out all the stops for Christmas in Romance.

Between odd animals, lost loves, second chances, hidden identities, a secret Santa, and bickering senior citizens, it might just take a miracle to bring everyone a happily-ever-after for the holidays.

Settle in a chair by the fire, sip a cup of hot cocoa, and immerse yourself in the friendly town of Romance with this series of six sweet Christmas novellas from bestselling and award-winning authors.

Sleigh Bells Ring in Romance by Shanna Hatfield - A determined widow and a persistent rancher need a nudge toward love.

A Merry Miracle in Romance by Melanie D. Snitker - It'll take a Christmas miracle to turn a grudging friendship into true love.

Holding Onto Love in Romance by Liwen Y. Ho - A small town inn owner and a big time pop star need a reason to keep holding onto love.

A Reel Christmas in Romance by J. J. DiBenedetto - Unwittingly engaged in the plot of a classic Hollywood romance, can two email pen-pals find their way to a happy ending?

A Christmas Carol in Romance by Franky A. Brown - A bitter-on-love radio DJ and his girlfriend of romance past need a second chance.

Santa's Visit in Romance by Jessica L. Elliott - Santa's got his work cut out for him to help a reluctant couple find love during the holidays.

Find out more about
Romance, Oregon on Facebook:
https://www.facebook.com/welcometoromance/

Acknowledgments

I'm so thankful for the wonderful authors of this series. Shanna, Franky, Liwen, James, and Jess, it has truly been a blessing. I cannot express how much I appreciate you!

Many thanks to Jennifer at Jennifer Pitts Photography for the gorgeous photo, and to Shanna Hatfield for creating the beautiful cover for *A Merry Miracle in Romance*. This book would not be complete if it weren't for the editing talent of Heather Hayden, and the hawk eyes of my amazing beta readers. Steph and Denny, you ladies are fabulous!

Most of all, I am in awe of the true meaning of Christmas. Thank you, Father, for sending us the gift of your son, Jesus.

About the Author

Melanie D. Snitker has enjoyed writing fiction for as long as she can remember. She started out creating episodes of cartoon shows she wanted to see as a child, and her love of writing grew from there. She and her husband live in Texas with their two children, who keep their lives full of adventure, and two dogs, who add a dash of mischief to the family dynamics. In her spare time, Melanie enjoys photography, reading, crocheting, baking, and hanging out with family and friends.

http://www.melaniedsnitker.com
https://twitter.com/MelanieDSnitker
https://www.facebook.com/melaniedsnitker

Subscribe to Melanie's newsletter and receive a monthly e-mail containing recipes, information about new releases, giveaways, and more! You can find a link to sign up on her website.

Books by Melanie D. Snitker

I Still Do
(Second Chance With You Book 6)

Calming the Storm
(A Marriage of Convenience)

Love's Compass Series:
Finding Peace (Book 1)
Finding Hope (Book 2)
Finding Courage (Book 3)
Finding Faith (Book 4)
Finding Joy (Book 5)
Finding Grace (Book 6)

Life Unexpected Series:
Safe In His Arms (Book 1)
Someone to Trust (Book 2)

Welcome to Romance
Finding Forever in Romance
A Merry Miracle in Romance

Brides of Clearwater Series:
Marrying Mandy (Book 1)
Marrying Raven (Book 2)
Marrying Chrissy (Book 3)

www.ingramcontent.com/pod-product-compliance
Lightning Source LLC
Chambersburg PA
CBHW052006220626
47052CB00004B/1119